I0685821

MUSHROOM HONEYMOON

BOOK TWO IN THE PSYCHEDELIC LOVE SERIES

CHARLOTTE K. DUNE

OCEAN FLOWER PRESS

Publisher's Note:

This is a work of fiction. Names, characters, places and incidents either are the product of the author's imagination or are used fictitiously and any resemblance to actual persons, living or dead, events, or locales is entirely coincidental.

ISBN: 978-1-7343089-5-2

Distributed by Ocean Flower Press.

Cover Models: Nathaniel Cinelli and Jeanine Lamounette

Cover and insert art by Giulio Villa

Additional insert art by Rodrigo Nunez

Mushroom ornamental sketches by Isys Mulira

Saman and Thelma — Illustration by Giulio Villa

FOREWORD

Mushroom Honeymoon is the second book in the *Psychedelic Love Series*.

Other books in this series:
    Book 1: *Cactus Friends: A Psychedelic Love Story*
    Book 3: *Hawaii Ayahuasca* (to be released)

This book does not condone the use or distribution of illegal drugs, but it encourages the legalization, research, and decriminalization of beneficial and healing, entheogenic plants.

To support research and the decriminalization of entheogens please visit M.A.P.S., the Multidisciplinary Association for Psychedelic Studies at https://maps.org/

And let's stay in touch!

Email me, or subscribe to my newsletter and get a free entheogenic reading guide.

Grab your free *Entheogenic Reading Guide* here:
    https://charlottedune.com/entheogenic-reading-list/

Thank you so much for reading!

— Charlotte Dune

To Ann, for being my guide to Hawaii.

Every pain and every joy, every thought and sigh... must return to you — all in the same succession and sequence — even this spider and this moonlight between the trees and even this moment and I myself. The eternal hourglass of existence is turned over again and again—and you with it, speck of dust.

— Frederick Nietzsche

1

The veins in Saman's arm bulged as his old, contaminated blood exited him, and the new, cleaned-up blood flowed into his body. The tubes of the dialysis machine saved his life today, as they'd done, three times a week, every week, for the past ten years. Above him, on the TV mounted to the wall of the Dialysis Center, the Miami morning news played — a shooting in Hialeah, a free-breakfast program for families living in motels, and a harsher penalty for people caught texting and driving. He closed his eyes and exhaled. When this was all over, he wanted to leave South Florida for a while, to go somewhere quiet and full of trees, away from sirens and commercials. Almost every summer he felt this way; the intense heat, tourists, endless traffic, and constant high-rise construction wore on his nerves.

Adrienne, the morning dialysis attendant, came to his bed and put her hands on her hips. "So, any big plans after the transplant? I'm sure it'll be a relief not to need this place anymore."

"It will be a relief, but I'll miss you guys," he said, giving her a smile.

Adrienne tossed her long, black box braids over her shoulder and laughed, "That's what they all say, but no one ever comes back to visit. You spend hours and years with people and then they disappear."

"Nope, not me," Saman said. "I'll come back and say hi." As much as he wanted to never need dialysis again, he'd also grown accustomed to his routine. The center felt like home. He enjoyed coming every other day, joking with Adrienne and zoning out while the machines converted him from run-down to energized again.

"Seriously, what's the first thing you want to do after you recover?"

Saman smiled, "Well, I'm going to take my wife on our honeymoon."

"Oooh right, I forgot about the honeymoon. Where y'all gonna go?"

"Hawaii." Saman raised his eyebrows, "From one hot place to another."

"Hawaii? Y'all realize Jamaica is like right there?" She pointed to the south.

Saman shrugged, "Well, Thelma always wanted to see Hawaii, so that's where we're going."

"Alrighty then," Adrienne said, "Gotta give the wifey what she wants!"

"Yep, my sister's husband told me the key to a good marriage is just two words, 'Yes, honey.'"

"Damn straight, Thelma is a lucky lady. You better post some photos, 'cause, Lord knows, my husband isn't taking me to Hawaii anytime soon."

Saman grinned, "I could do without the million-hour flight, but at least I'll be able to travel again." Since his kidney problem developed, now almost a decade ago, he'd only traveled once, for a friend's wedding in California, but between the jet lag and the treks through San Francisco to the dialysis center, he hadn't enjoyed the trip. Hawaii, he promised himself, would be different. It was hard to imagine having the freedom to go and keep going, without needing his blood pressure checked, without dialysis. Already he regretted buying their new house, thinking they should have spent the money on travel instead. He wanted to visit Thailand and India.

"And what about after the honeymoon? Will you stay at the radio station?" Adrienne asked.

"I don't know. I need to figure that out. I want to travel more, and I'd love to go back to University; I never finished my undergrad, but at my age, I don't know..." he paused, "Plus, it's so expensive."

"Well, life isn't all about money. You know that." She gestured at the tubes connected to his olive-skinned arm.

"Yeah, but we just bought a house."

"What would you study if you went back?"

Saman shrugged, he considered her question before responding. He'd stumbled on a documentary about a team at Cornell that used ocean audio recordings to predict fish behavior and to create sonic representations of everything from bacteria to coral reef degradation. The field of bioacoustics, the study of how animals and plants communicated sonically and how sound impacted the environment interested him. But what money was there in a field like that? What kind of job would he be able to get with a bioacoustics degree, other than a teaching or research position? And that was if he was lucky. Plus, he was too old to be someone's lab intern. Still, if the surgery went well, he wanted to get an underwater mic to record aquatic sounds.

Adrienne waited for his answer.

"Maybe computer programming," he said, deciding he didn't want to explain the concept of bioacoustics.

"I bet that pays well. You know, my sister went to FIU for Marine Biology at age thirty-eight. We all thought she was nuts. Her husband almost divorced her, he was so mad at her for quitting her nursing job, and they had two kids in middle school."

"Did she finish?"

"She sure did, and now she works in Key West for a foundation saving the coral reefs, and she's happy as a clam." Adrienne laughed, "No pun intended."

"Wow," Saman said, "but that's a rare story, I think."

"I guess, but life is long. People have like ten careers these days."

"That's true." Maybe going back to school wasn't a pipe dream. Though he probably couldn't get into Cornell, much less pay the tuition or convince Thelma to move to New York. She hated the cold weather and he'd put her through enough already; it wasn't fair to ask her for more sacrifices when her own art career was booming.

A petite Cuban woman named Dolores, the receptionist of the dialysis center, came behind Adrienne. "Your final session, Saman, I can hardly believe it. How are you feeling about the transplant? When is it, in a few days right?"

"Yes, on Friday. Just hoping it all goes well."

"It will," Adrienne said. "And you'll feel amazing once you recover."

"Thanks, yeah I'm actually seeing my donor this afternoon with another friend of ours," Saman added.

"Oh wonderful. I'm so excited for you," Dolores said. "We also got you a little something," she winked. "Don't move. I'll be right back."

"I can't go anywhere yet," Saman called after her, pointing to the tube in his arm. After every session he had to wait to ensure that his blood pressure remained steady post-treatment.

From a nearby bed, hooked to his own dialysis machine, an older man with a potbelly watched Saman. "You getting out of here?" he asked, as if the dialysis center was a prison.

Saman nodded, "I am."

"Send me some of your good luck, will ya?"

"Will do." Saman didn't recognize the man, which was a shame. He'd hoped to see some other morning regulars — a grandmother with severe diabetes named Anna, and a man in his mid-forties named Frank, who had a rare, but treatable kidney disease. Whenever he didn't see a regular at the center, he feared the worst, which wasn't unrealistic, given the dire health consequences of end-stage renal failure.

Dolores came back holding a gift bag and a card. "From all of us here," she said.

"You guys didn't have to do this." Saman took the bag. "I'm the one who should be giving you a gift."

He opened the envelope first. It was a large stock card with the hospital's branding, but inside was a picture of the entire staff of the center smiling and waving. Everyone had signed the card, and written their well-wishes, including Frank and Anna. Inside the bag was a mug from the Dialysis Center, some gourmet coffee, and fancy spoons made of chocolate.

Adrienne grinned, "We know you missed your coffee, and now you'll be able to drink it again!"

"This is perfect. Thank you so much for this and for everything you've done for me." Saman swallowed, moved by their affection.

"Ahh," Adrienne said, "You're gonna make me cry."

The two ladies came on each side of the bed and hugged him. He returned their embrace and squeezed his eyes shut, holding back a flood of emotional relief that had been building for weeks.

"Don't make me cry too." He patted them on the shoulder, and let out a nervous laugh, "Like I said, I'll be back."

Adrienne and Dolores squeezed him again, then unhooked him from the dialyzer for the last time.

SAMAN LINGERED on the sidewalk in front of the dialysis center. The yellow, single-story cement structure looked small, like he'd already outgrown it. Storm clouds brewed behind the building, turning the sky dark gray. *I should feel relieved*, he thought, but instead, he felt something else. He took a deep breath and got in his car.

Skipping the highway, he navigated northwest in silence, to their new home in Fort Lauderdale. Fat drops of rain smacked against the windshield and thunder boomed in the distance. The drive felt somber, not like an accomplishment, but like a departure. *So much is about to change*. He wouldn't need dialysis after the transplant, but he'd be immunocompromised. Transplant patients had to take immunosuppressants for the rest of their lives, to keep their new kidney from being attacked as a foreign invader.

Stopping at a red light, something his mother said earlier that week lingered in his mind like dust on a shelf. "Now you can leave that awful dialysis place behind, with all those poor people, and focus on moving up at the radio station." His mother had said.

The comment bothered him — first, because his mother thought the center was awful; second, because he never defined the other patients as "poor people"; and third, because his mother had never suggested that he try for a promotion at the radio station.

The light turned green. Had his mother expected him to die? He frowned. But what did she expect now? There weren't any better positions for him at the station. He crawled behind a line of cars to the next stoplight. *I should have taken the highway*, he thought.

The downpour increased in intensity. A disheveled, deeply tanned, older man carrying a black umbrella and a bucket full of roses walked between the stopped vehicles. *He shouldn't be out in this storm*. Whenever it rained in Florida, lightning followed.

The man held a clump of red roses covered in clear plastic. Saman made eye contact, to show respect, but shook his head, "no."

"For your wife," the man yelled.

Thunder cracked overhead. The rose dealer rapped on the window with his knuckle. "Ten dollars for two?"

I could get one for Rita and one for Maria, Saman thought. He'd see both of them that afternoon for a private magic mushroom ceremony, a gift from Maria to him and Rita before the special day of the kidney operation. The flowers would be a nice gift and something to adorn the ceremony's altar. He fished out his wallet from his back pocket. The only thing inside was a fifty-dollar bill. Saman cracked the window. "Do you have change?"

"Yes. I have." The man passed two red roses to Saman.

"I'll take white ones, please," Saman said.

The man swapped the flowers and handed him the white roses. Saman gave the man his fifty-dollar bill and the man bolted across the street with the cash.

"Hey, wait, my change!" Saman yelled.

The running man did not look back.

Saman scowled. Then again, it was pouring rain; maybe he would have done the same if he was desperate enough to sell roses in a thunderstorm? But Saman wasn't in a financial position to hand out fifty-dollar bills. Between paying off the mortgage on Rita's house, a gift to thank her for donating her kidney, and the purchase of their own house, he'd be in debt forever.

The man sat at the covered bus stop across the street, acting as if nothing had happened.

The stoplight turned green, and lightning cracked overhead. In his side mirror, Saman caught the man walking to the other side of the street, to target the next round of cars. *I guess he needs the money more than I do.* Saman glanced at the roses. The flowers weren't worth fifty dollars, but Rita and Maria would like them.

He switched on a bluegrass band called *Doggy Bowl*, and tapped the steering wheel in rhythm with the drums, singing along.

> *"Hammer girl, hammer down the house.*
> *Gonna tear these old walls out and make*
> *something else."*

As he drove, Saman concentrated on the mushroom ceremony. Maria advised setting an intention before eating the sacred fungi. *I could focus on finding the right next step in my life*, he thought. Though it was hard to see beyond the transplant, and his recovery could take six, even eight weeks. "Just get me through this alive," he murmured, and turned up the volume on his music, louder and louder, until it blocked the roar of the storm outside.

2

By the kitchen window, Thelma unbraided her shoulder-length blonde hair and wrapped a brown sweater tighter around her thin frame. The July thunderstorm flooded the sky with rain. In the front yard, puddles formed, and palm fronds flapped in the wind. A miniature waterfall cascaded off their roof's awning and every few minutes the house flashed with blue light.

Thelma reached for the sink's faucet to fill a kettle with water, then stopped. *Was it safe to run water during a lightning storm?* Bathtubs she knew were dangerous because lightning could go through the pipes and shock the bather, but what about a sink? She quickly filled the electric kettle and plugged it into the wall before another rod of electricity hit.

As she waited for the water to boil, Thelma opened a box on the counter and pulled out a hand-thrown clay teacup, painted gray with an ocean-blue rim, a wedding gift from her cousin. Unpacked cardboard boxes still dotted various rooms of her new house. *Our house*, she reminded herself. Sometimes Thelma forgot she was married. Everything had happened so fast — the wedding, the move, her art shows, Saman's deteriorating health...

The kettle button turned red, and she poured a cup of lemon and ginger tea. Stirring honey into the mug, she sighed. She preferred coffee, but they would soon have a mushroom ceremony with Maria and caffeine was unadvisable. She fingered the string of her tea bag. *Is having a ceremony before the surgery really a good idea?* The last thing she wanted was for the procedure to be delayed again. They'd already rescheduled the kidney transplant twice, once because Rita was sick, and again because Saman wasn't well enough to proceed. Doctor's appointments replaced lunch dates and the first months of their marriage hadn't been a honeymoon.

Flipping over the small piece of paper attached to the tea bag's string, Thelma read the inscription: *Good ideas are like cups of tea, brew until ready.* She frowned; the words had no meaning for her at the moment. She suspected that Saman wanted the ceremony because he was worried about dying during the transplant. Psychedelic experiences often quelled those concerns. A brush with the beyond made death more acceptable. Saman hoped the mushrooms would calm his mind and center him and Rita before the surgery. Maria had agreed, albeit with the stipulation that he take a low dose.

As Thelma sipped her tea, she observed how the rain's wetness accentuated the natural colors of the flower beds edging the front of their house. *I should get my camera and take some micro-lens pictures of the plant textures*, she thought.

Saman pulled into the driveway, interrupting her ideas. His gray cat, StanGetz, ran to the front door like a dog to meet his master. StanGetz still hadn't warmed to Thelma. Sometimes the animal stared at her, like "Who the hell are you, lady?" He never sat on her lap or rubbed against her leg.

"Hey," Saman said, holding a gift bag, two white roses, and a wet umbrella.

"Oh, that's so sweet babe. I love them" Thelma said, taking the flowers.

Saman hesitated, "Oops sorry, I actually got those for Maria and Rita."

Thelma hesitated, feeling silly. "Of course, sorry, that's sweet, too."

"No, you're right, I should've gotten one for you." He slipped off his sneakers and put them by the door, still holding the dripping umbrella. "I don't know why I didn't ask for three."

"That's okay. Here, I'll put that under the overhang to dry," Thelma said, pointing to the umbrella.

Saman shrugged, "I was going to put it in the sink."

Thelma blinked. *The sink?*

She followed him to the kitchen, where he placed the dripping-wet umbrella, half-open, into the kitchen sink. "The center gave me a bunch of goodbye gifts too."

"That was nice of them," Thelma said, staring at the umbrella in the sink. While it made sense to her that wet things could dry in a sink, the object looked like it was in the wrong place. Sometimes Saman did weird things, strange habits that she didn't understand or expect, like eating soup for breakfast, or thinking it was disgusting when she left her shoes in their bedroom instead of by the front door. *Were these quirks his own personality, or a result of his Persian upbringing, examples of their cultural differences?*

She stared at the umbrella a second longer, then let it go. "Have you spoken to Maria or Rita? Do you think she'll still want to do the ceremony?"

"No, but I assume they're still coming. Why? You want to cancel?"

"No. Do you?" Thelma asked, half-hoping he would say yes. "I didn't know with this weather."

"Maybe call Rita and see what she thinks?"

"Okay."

Saman gave her a peck on the cheek, then left to change his clothes.

Maria kept the ceremony on schedule. They would move inside.

Thelma set about creating a welcoming space in their living room. She pushed back the furniture — a white sofa and coffee table, moved from her old condo, and a black, mid-modern leather recliner Saman loved. When he got home from work, he would sit in the chair and pet StanGetz before doing anything else.

Saman returned, wearing khaki shorts and a worn Herbie Hancock t-shirt left over from when he worked as a roadie, before he got sick. The fistula for his dialysis treatment bulged like a fisherman's rope under the skin on his right forearm.

"I could have moved the sofa for you," he said.

"That's okay. It wasn't heavy." Thelma lit candles and Saman arranged silk cloth and colorful crystals on the table, along with a potted, white and purple-spotted orchid and the two roses. They unrolled decorative blankets and placed throw pillows around the table, facing the makeshift altar. Dimming the overhead lights, Saman turned on meditative shamanic music. The space was ready.

They sat on the floor, their backs to the sofa, legs outstretched. Saman traced her thigh with his fingers, "I love you so much." He gazed at her and she kissed him on the lips, a soft kiss with their mouths closed.

"I love you, too." She whispered and rested her head on his shoulder, letting the pure bliss of their love absorb into her body like rain. She always liked to relax before ceremonies.

They didn't wait long before the doorbell rang, and Maria came in like a gust of wind.

"My loves!" she said and hugged Thelma and Saman. "Eh, this crazy weather! Couldn't it have waited till we were done?"

"Do you need help with anything?" Saman asked.

"Yes, yes, can you grab my suitcase? The car's unlocked." She patted Saman on the shoulder, then smoothed her black hair, made frizzy by the humidity. Maria's brown eyes scanned the house. "Rita isn't here yet?" she asked, slipping off her wet rain jacket.

"Not yet."

"Hmm. I thought she'd beat me here." Maria frowned.

"Shall I take this to the living room?" Saman asked, returning with Maria's rolling suitcase.

"Yes please, dear."

Maria wore a long, cream-colored, linen dress with a bright blue cardigan, and soft, neutral makeup that gave her a youthful appearance, though she was old enough to be Thelma's mother. As she entered the living room, Maria stopped to admire Thelma's now-famous portrait of Saman with his body covered in feathers. The portrait hung in a thick teak frame on their wall. "Oh my, that looks stunning there, really lovely," Maria exclaimed.

"Thank you," Thelma said. "I'll sell it eventually, but I'm not ready to part with it quite yet, though Saman says it makes him feel vain to have a giant picture of himself in the house."

"Nonsense!" Maria said. "It's a masterpiece."

"From a master artist," Saman added.

Thelma blushed. "Okay, enough you two."

They helped Maria arrange items on their homemade altar — a small clay pot, a blue glass bottle with water in it, a sage smudge, stationary, and a few pens. From her suitcase, she removed an interlocking stack of quartz healing sound bowls in different colors, layered like Russian dolls and arranged everything in a semi-circle, facing where the group would lie down for the ceremony.

"How are you feeling?" Maria asked Saman.

"Good. Excited. I just came from dialysis, so that helps."

"Perfect, well I'm going easy on you today." Maria placed three pieces of chocolate on a plate, each in the shape of a rose, then dusted them with a fine, dark brown powder. "*Lion's mane* and *reishi* mushrooms — I mix the nutritional mushrooms with the magic ones," she winked.

"Sounds delicious," Saman said.

"I have a special one for you," Maria replied, pulling out a white chocolate rose from a small Tupperware container.

"Oh, what a coincidence," Saman said, "I got white roses for you and Rita." He gestured to the flowers. "This is for you."

"You are too sweet, but you know there are no coincidences? The white rose symbolizes transformation and new beginnings."

"That's a beautiful meaning."

"Now, where is Ms. Rita?" Maria asked.

Thelma checked the time, it was thirty minutes past when they'd said to arrive, but Rita was often late. She once arrived so late to Thelma's art show that she missed the entire event and found them loading the car in the parking lot.

"She should be here by now." Saman frowned.

Thelma knew Saman well enough to tell that he was fretting about something but trying not to show it. He looked uneasy. *Was he nervous about taking the mushrooms? Or worried about Rita?*

"I'll call her," Maria said. "I want to start so I'm not driving home too late."

Rita didn't answer.

"She probably didn't pick up because she's driving," Thelma said. Rita was on her way from Orlando, about a three-hour trip from Fort Lauderdale.

"Sure." Saman paced back and forth in front of the sofa. Thelma motioned for him to sit beside her on the ground, but he kept standing.

"Ugh," Maria said frustrated, "She has your new address, right?"

"Yes, I sent it to her." Thelma said.

They couldn't start without Rita. There was nothing to do but wait. Maria made small talk, but the mood grew more restless with each clap of thunder, and every minute that passed without Rita's arrival.

Thelma tried to call Rita again, but this time it went straight to voicemail.

"Maybe Rita changed her mind." Saman's eyes brimmed with concern.

"No way," Maria said. "She wouldn't do that."

"She's probably stuck in traffic from the rain," Thelma offered.

Another thirty minutes passed. The storm continued. Thelma brought everyone ice water with slices of lemon. They were now almost two hours behind schedule.

"I'm really worried." Maria said.

"Should I look for her?" Saman asked.

"Look for her where? I don't think it's a good idea to drive in this rain." Thelma furrowed her brow.

"She could be in an accident," Saman said.

"Should we put out an Amber alert or something?" Maria asked.

"I think that's only for kids," Thelma replied. "It's a silver alert, for, um..." she stopped, not wanting to call Rita an old person. "For an adult," she clarified, "and I don't know if," but before she could finish her sentence, the doorbell rang.

Saman bolted to the foyer. Thelma and Maria followed. Rita came inside, soaking wet.

"¡Dios mío!" Maria exclaimed, grabbing Rita's wet body and squeezing her. "We thought you were in an accident! What happened?"

Rita shook her head, "I'm so sorry. I was stuck in a flood and then I got lost. My phone died and I forgot my charger. Thankfully, I remembered the name of the street, so I asked for directions at a gas station, and they didn't know. Finally, I found someone who knew this street. It was a nightmare! And in all this rain." She waived her hands in the air. "Thank God, I remembered what Maria's car looked like or else I would never have found the house."

"I'm so glad you're okay." Thelma took Rita's wet jacket and hung it beside Maria's.

"I was so afraid I'd get stuck in the flood." Rita shook her head and blinked back tears.

"Shhh. Shhh," Maria said, rubbing Rita's back. "Everything's okay now."

"That's terrible," Saman said, "I'm so sorry. I guess we should have postponed." Saman embraced Rita. "I'm so glad you made it."

"Yes, yes, my dear boy." She hugged him back. "No, it's okay. I'm happy to see you. I should charge my phone. Juan is coming later today, and he will drive me." Rita smoothed out her skirt and top. "We're staying at his cousin's in Miami until the transplant. Actually, can I leave my car here?"

"Of course," Thelma said. "I'm so glad Juan will be with you." She gave Rita another hug.

"Now I really need this ceremony," Maria mumbled. "Come on, my loves. Let's get this boat rowing." And she motioned for them to follow her to the living room.

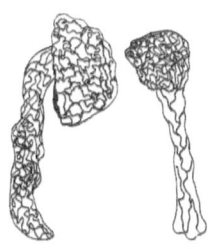

EYES CLOSED, Thelma relaxed on the floor, covered in a light teal blanket, listening to the soft harmonies of Maria's crystal singing bowl. After the stress of Rita's ordeal, she wanted to sink into the ceremony, to float away on the sound waves. The mushrooms would kick in soon, and transport her to another dimension, a place of uncertainty and dreams, of pleasure and magic. Though she knew some people had 'bad trips' on *psilocybin*, the active compound in the mushrooms, she herself had never experienced anything negative from the plant. The fungus was heart-opening and mind-expanding.

Maria spoke in a low, soothing voice, "Clear your consciousness of any events, past or future, any stresses or anxieties you're holding. Let them go. Stay in the present moment. Experience my words and your own body's sensations, the sounds, the fabric on your skin."

Thelma exhaled and her limbs tingled with anticipation. Fuzzy socks hugged her feet. It amazed her that Maria, who also ate the mushroom chocolates, could speak, sing, and play the bowls, as if unaffected by the psychedelics.

Opening one eye, Thelma peeked over at Saman. He looked peaceful under his blanket.

"Let the sounds wash over you from your legs to your spine. There is a warm, red light enveloping your hips, inside your lower groin, filling your roots," Maria said, holding a lit bunch of sage, circulating the fragrant smoke.

Thelma envisioned the red glow. It traveled through her pelvis, caressed her navel, and brought a tingling sensation to the folds of her pubic area.

Maria continued, "Today, we will focus on your root Chakra, before this special time, the transplant ceremony between Rita and Saman, a gift of life and connection. Let the red light run from your roots to your stomach, your liver, your kidneys, your appendix, washing your intestines, your blood, let it fill you with strength, with survival. It's a warm fire; let it burn away your fear."

The words flittered around Thelma like an echo in a stone cave. The magic mushrooms kicked in and coursed through her chest, arms, and legs. Her body was hot, then cool. The red light ran to her forehead.

As the intensity of the mushrooms increased, her skin fluttered with sensation like someone was pouring sand over her. An inner force squeezed her muscles. Her shoulder blades tightened. Energy bloomed from a tiny bud attached to the base of her spine and spread through her backside. It made her want to move or dance. She clenched her quadriceps as tightly as she could, lifting herself a fraction of a centimeter off the carpet, releasing the tension systematically. The blanket bunched under her lower back from all her squirming. *I need to move*, Thelma thought, *but it will be rude to get up during Maria's ceremony*. So, Thelma focused on the music, which turned into a red, transparent gas, then stabilized and became a thick tendril, a dark-violet vine, like an umbilical cord wrapping around her. The fibers constricted her spinal discs. Triangles and geometric shapes refracted like sparkling prisms of color. She moved outside her own body, now looking at someone else's intestines, someone else's ribs. A beating heart pulsed in the middle, in a puddle of blood and bones.

She examined the wet organ like a coroner. *Was she imagining Saman's transplant?* A shadowy circle in the center moved and bulged. *What was it?* The membrane broke and a round pod emerged, then rotated, revealing a tiny creature's body, connected by long, segmented legs. It inched toward her like a fiddler crab. She realized it was a spider, a blood-soaked, palm-sized spider with no face, only crimson, fur-covered fangs. A silk string connected it to the flesh below. Lowering its head, the arachnid bit into the heart.

Thelma's eyes snapped open; her trip jolted out of its flow by the disturbing image of the spider. Her stomach churned and for a moment she felt dizzy. Back in the living room, the overhead fan flickered in a hundred pieces, distorting in slow-motion like a zoetrope, spinning still images to form a film of shadows on the ceiling. She watched the fan rotate for what felt like hours. Several times she tried to close her eyes again, only to see the same image — gurgling fluids, cut flesh, pulsing organs, and the spider, its brown, coarse tusks, eye-less face, an abdomen like a blood-filled tick. *This is a strange trip*, she thought, no longer able to enjoy herself, too disturbed by the scene on loop beyond her logical mind.

Maria played a Native American flute beside the altar. The summer sun replaced the storm outside. Late afternoon light cast a ray of gold across Rita. Despite her age, Rita had been excited about doing the mushrooms, sensing that it was a special opportunity to bond with Saman before the transplant process. *What a blessing Rita is,* Thelma thought. Love and gratitude flooded through Thelma's body, and she wanted to hug everyone in the room. She watched Saman wake up, admiring his angular jaw, his pointed, hawk-like nose, and his five o'clock shadow. He looked more handsome than ever to her in that moment.

"Welcome back," Maria said, "Take your time."

Saman grinned at Thelma and she scooted beside him, folding herself into the crook of his arm. "You okay?" She whispered.

"Yeah, are you?" He kissed her on the forehead.

"Yes." She relaxed against his chest. This was the first plant medicine they'd eaten together since the *wachuma* ceremony where they first met.

After a few minutes, Rita also woke up, "Oh my, I'm late for the party." She giggled.

"That is your trend for today," Maria said.

They all laughed.

"Our inner-children are still here," Maria chuckled, "bringing their mirth and mischief. That is what the children's medicine does."

It made Thelma happy to see Rita having fun, her stressful drive forgotten.

Maria held a flat drum in the air and struck it with a mallet, singing, "Thank you, *medicina*, from my heart, we love you so much. We love you so much." She repeated the melody and words several times, then placed the drum on the altar. "Let's share any memorable experiences or insights you gained. Saman, my son, please go first."

Saman nodded, the mood in the room switched to serious. He twisted his long black hair into a man-bun and secured it with an elastic band from around his wrist. "I didn't see too much," he said, "but I thought about the future." He faced Rita. "And about what you're doing for me, giving me something so precious." He paused, "Not to get emotional — but I'm tremendously grateful, and I deeply appreciate you and your gift."

Rita hung on his words, with kindness in her eyes. She held her hands to her heart. "You will make me cry."

"I've been carrying a lot of fear," Saman continued, "Maria, when you were describing the colors, I only saw black, and I realized it was my fear." He turned again to Rita, "I keep expecting the worst, like when you were late today, I thought you'd decided not to come, like you'd changed your mind about the kidney transplant, and weren't..." he sucked in air, clenching his lips together, overwhelmed by his own confession.

"Oh, no, Saman, my dear, I'd never do that to you." Rita scooted to him on her knees, looking too formal for the bohemian setting in her black slacks and button-down red blouse. She hugged Saman. "I'd never do that," she repeated.

"I know," Saman said, letting go of Rita. "I need to stop worrying and accept that my luck has turned." He grinned, "Accept that everything will be okay, instead of constantly waiting for the other shoe to drop."

"That's true," Maria said, "There's no need to fear the worst, or to expect anything, good or bad. The future is unknown and uncontrollable by us. In that unknowing there's release and grace, surrender and acceptance."

"I won't squander this opportunity," Saman added, "and I felt a strong desire to create something meaningful, to do something useful for the world after I recover from the surgery."

"I know you will," Rita said.

Thelma's heart expanded with affection for Saman. Everything would be better after the transplant. *This is the beginning of a new Saman,* she thought.

"Thank you for sharing that, my son," Maria said, then turned to Rita, "You're next, dear."

"Well," Rita said, sliding to the opposite side of the circle, "I felt very free, and happy, like I was a child, and I saw myself in the body of a *Wayúu* woman. It was strange. I was selling *mochilas* along the roadside. Do you know those women?" she paused, remembering the trip. "But it was very nice." She met Thelma's eyes. "And I'm so glad you invited me. I'll never forget this day. Thank you."

"I know the Wayúu women, of course." Maria said. She made her *namaste*-gesture at Rita.

"What's that?" Thelma asked.

"The Wayúu are an indigenous people in Colombia. The women weave beautiful handbags and colorful blankets," Maria answered. "What a lovely image, Rita, you must reflect on that and let us know what you think it means."

"I will. I'm not sure yet," Rita said. "Maybe it was calling me to visit Colombia. You know, my late husband was Colombian, but I haven't been since he passed."

"I think so." Maria winked then turned to Thelma. "And you, my dear? I saw you squirming. Were you having a difficult time?"

Thelma swallowed, that was an understatement. "Yes,

sort of. I don't know why." She hesitated, then described the spider and the heart.

"Oh, man," Saman said, rubbing her shoulder, "I didn't realize you were having a bad trip."

"I don't know if I'd call it bad, but it was strange."

"A spider, very interesting." Maria rubbed her chin. "The Wayúu say a spider taught the women how to weave the mochilas that Rita saw in her vision. It's like a Colombian Rumpelstiltskin story."

"Really?" Rita said, "That is a coincidence."

Thelma raised her eyebrows; her spider was far from a fairy tale.

"*Sí*, let's look up what spiders represent in my book," Maria said. From her tote bag, she pulled out a thick, old book, bound in a worn, dark-green leather cover. "Okay, let's see." She flipped through the pages, then showed them an illustration of a tarantula-like spider, resting on a web of dense, intersecting ink lines. "It says because spiders catch creatures in webs, they symbolize that you feel trapped."

Thelma tilted her head to the side. "Hmmm... I don't really feel trapped. Does it say anything else?"

Saman leaned back on his elbows, listening.

"Freud wrote that spiders represented the maternal. It also says spiders have been on earth for 300 million years, so they signify ancient wisdom."

"That sounds good," Saman said.

Thelma leaned deeper into Saman's side. Though she loved Maria's little book of animals, she felt drained and ready for everyone to leave so she and Saman could cuddle in bed.

"I've never cared for spiders myself," Rita interjected, making an ew-face.

"No, me neither," Thelma said, yawning. "My 6th grade science class had a tarantula that escaped from its cage. I spent the rest of the year afraid it would crawl into my hair."

"Here, I like this one." Maria ran her hand along the page, "The Hopi tribe believed in a Grandmother Spider Goddess, called *Kokyangwuti,* who wove the matrix of life that created our reality. She changed forms between an old woman and a spider who lived underground. When the Hopi needed help, they called her, and she guided them to their higher purposes. They believed one day Grandmother Spider would pull all her creations back to a central source." Maria looked from the book at Thelma, "This applies to you dear; it says this cosmic spider's webs connected all reality, and by navigating the webs, one can harness psychic and telepathic abilities."

Thelma nodded, taking in Maria's words, though they didn't resonate with her vision.

"Oh yeah," Saman joined the conversation, excitement rising in his voice, "I remember a Persian story about a spider woman. My uncle scared us with it as kids. There was an old lady named 'Al,' and she had red eyes and long pointed teeth, and two giant pet spiders that sat on her shoulders, and she would. . ." he stopped.

An emotion Thelma couldn't place clouded Saman's expression.

"She would what?" Maria asked.

"Okay, this is creepy that I've thought of this today. . . I haven't thought about this in decades." Saman shook his head, "Man, I almost don't want to say it."

"Say what?" Thelma was breathless. Something about the tone of his voice made her anxious.

Rita leaned forward, "Well, you have to finish the story now."

Saman inhaled, his chest rising, "Al stole people's hearts

and organs while they slept, then carried them in a basket back to her demon dimension where she fed the organs to her pet spiders."

His words stood stiff in the room like a wooden door. Thelma's mouth went dry. The image of the spider crawled in her mind, the long, segmented legs, the blood-covered fangs, a half-spun web. She shuddered. Reality felt fractured. *I'm still tripping on the mushrooms,* she thought, and suddenly she wanted to open all the windows in the room, to allow her feelings to escape.

"My word," Maria said, breaking the silence. "What a terrible thing to tell a child."

3

Under the thin hospital gown, Saman's heartbeat accelerated, his breath was jagged, as if he'd run up a flight of steps. The warmth of Thelma's palm on his forearm did little to calm the fear circulating through his chest like smoke in a locked bedroom. *This is either the end of my troubles, or the beginning of my end.*

"You're doing great," Thelma said, rubbing his arm.

Did she hear my thoughts? Sometimes he wondered if Thelma could read his mind. Unusual exchanges passed between them without words, her intuition a force possessed by few.

Exhaling, Saman pulled the hospital sheet higher on his chest. His body shrunk as his kidneys weakened; he weighed less now at thirty-six than when he was thirteen. He swallowed, dry-mouthed from all the medication in his system.

A nurse in floral scrubs appeared on the other side of the stretcher with two male orderlies behind her. He forced himself to smile, to appear stoic. Nothing felt real.

"Are you ready?" the nurse asked.

"Yep." He gazed back at Thelma, "Here we go."

"Here we go," she repeated. Shadows encircled her blue eyes in the dull, fluorescent lighting. It was an early morning for both of them.

He squeezed her hand, "I love you."

"I love you, too," she replied. Leaning over, she kissed him once on the lips.

The orderlies wheeled Saman away on a stretcher, rattling down the hospital hallway, then took him up a few floors in a large, empty elevator. *What if something terrible happens to Rita because of me?* He wondered. *So many things could go wrong.*

He contemplated climbing off the stretcher. *Pull yourself together, man.*

They entered another room.

"How are you doing?" A plump nurse with glasses and brown hair asked.

"I'm good," he lied.

The orderlies positioned him against the wall, between two machines with computer monitors. White curtains hung from the ceiling, spaced out like shower stalls in a gym.

Behind him, another stretcher rolled into the room. Saman swiveled his head. It was Rita Cando. She waved and he waved back. Even in a hospital gown, Rita looked more like a Spanish movie star than a widow subsiding off social security payments.

"Morning," he said, trying to act normal as the nurse checked his blood pressure.

"Hola, mijo," Rita said. "You good?" She called him her son often in Spanish, though they were of no relation. He found it endearing.

"Yep. Have you changed your mind yet?"

"Me? I'm here for lipo," Rita winked.

He cracked a smile, "You don't need lipo."

"I told them, add a little right here while you're at it," Rita waved her hands over her breasts and giggled.

The nurse interrupted them, "The anesthesiologist will be in soon. Are you both comfortable?"

"Oh, already? *Sí, sí.* I'm ready." Rita put on a brave expression, but her voice quivered.

He'd never understand her generosity. When Saman's transplant coordinator had learned that Rita was not a family member, she'd shrugged, "You'd be surprised how many strangers walk in off the street and volunteer. It gives their lives meaning," she explained, "or some do it for financial reasons."

The comment haunted Saman. *Was Rita only doing this for the money?* But she'd responded to Thelma's Facebook post looking for a donor before they'd offered compensation. Rita said Saman resembled her late husband, who had passed away from pancreatic cancer. Thelma's artistic post about Saman's kidney situation had touched Rita. Still, Saman couldn't imagine volunteering to have surgery for a stranger, or even a new friend. His own sister had politely declined giving him one of her kidneys, and he couldn't blame her.

To further complicate Saman's feelings about the organ exchange, while it was illegal to buy and sell organs in Florida, once they determined that Rita was serious about the donation, and a good candidate in terms of health, Saman and Thelma had given Rita a substantial gift, paying down the mortgage on her house, freeing her from debt, as a thank you for the kidney.

The doctors claimed the risks for Rita were low, but Saman knew that the few possible complications were grave, and the more he got to know Rita, the more he adored her. Her tendency towards optimism was such a contrast to his own mother. Rita was like the fun aunt he'd never had. He wished they could pay for her house without needing to do the transplant in return.

Then again, as Thelma reminded him, the stakes were high — just his life.

The nurse pulled the curtain closed between them, and Saman took a deep breath, "You know, I'll never be able to thank you enough for this," he said in a quiet voice, as if confessing to a priest.

"Shhh, *mijo*." Rita shook her head. "No, no. You will make me cry. Shhh."

They waited in silence for the surgeon. Saman wished he'd worn socks; his feet were cold. An old, Persian lullaby drifted into his head.

Gonjishk la la, sanjaab la la, aamad dobareh, mahtaab la la
Sparrow go to sleep,
Squirrel go to sleep,
The moonlight shines again, go to sleep, go to sleep.

He'd forgotten that song, and his mother's habit of singing it as she tucked him into bed. Her voice had annoyed him as a child, but now it returned as a sweet memory. He focused on the melody, trying to halt his negative thoughts, but like a never-ending pinball game, as soon as one dropped, another shot up.

Please, let this work, he prayed. *Let Thelma and I live a long, healthy life. Please, don't let anything happen to Rita or me.*

A tall man with broad shoulders, dressed in surgical scrubs came into Saman's view. He had a military air, like an ex-marine.

"Good morning, I'll be your anesthesiologist today."

Saman nodded.

"I'm waiting for your surgical team to arrive," The man smiled, "then we'll get started."

The anesthesiologist flipped through Saman's chart, while the nurses filled out paperwork. As the surgical team arrived, Saman's pulse sped even faster. His palms oozed with sweat, and his stomach growled from fasting before the surgery. *Thelma's probably sitting next to my mother trying to make small talk.* His wife never knew what to say to his mother, and the feeling was mutual.

"Well, the day has come," the surgeon said, standing above Saman and adjusting his rubber gloves. "Do you have any last questions?"

Saman shook his head, no. He took a deep breath. *Calm down. Just calm the fuck down.*

"Don't be nervous. You're going to feel better than you've felt in a long time very soon." The doctor turned to the anesthesiologist, "He's all yours."

"I'm going to put this mask on you to start," the anesthesiologist said, as he fastened the plastic mask over Saman's mouth and nose. Then he adjusted a silver machine with tubes and a computer screen.

Let's get it over with, Saman squeezed his fists into balls.

"You're doing great," the anesthesiologist said. "Take some nice deep breaths."

The cold liquid entered his blood through the IV. As instructed, he sucked in air from the plastic mask, trying not to panic. *It's happening.*

"Now count backwards in your head from 10," the anesthesiologist said.

10, 9, 8, 7...

IN THE WAITING ROOM, Thelma shivered. The hospital was sub-arctic compared to the hot Miami sunshine outside. Saman's mother sat next to her, with a blank expression. They struggled to converse under normal circumstances, but she was grateful for his mother's silence this morning.

Rita Cando's boyfriend, Juan, leaned forward in an armchair to Thelma's left, looking down at his cell phone. His scalp peaked through thinning wisps of white hair. Liver spots covered his hands. He was friendly, but his English was as limited as Thelma's Spanish.

She crossed and uncrossed her legs, trying to read a *Newsweek* magazine, but reading the same paragraph over and over again — something about rising sea levels in coastal cities. She shuddered. The world seemed full of problems.

Laying the magazine on her lap, Thelma tugged her blond hair out of its ponytail, letting it drape on her shoulders, hoping to warm her cold neck. She'd said goodbye to Saman almost an hour ago. He must be in the operating room by now.

During the week before the operation, they'd tried to watch videos of the kidney transplant procedure together, but Thelma could not stomach the blood and the veins, the yellow fat and the unknown organs that looked like wet, bulging, brown balloons. So, Saman watched the videos by himself. He read countless articles on the recovery period and memorized all the worst and best possible outcomes of the transplant. The information made her more nervous, but he couldn't help himself; he needed to know.

Thelma prayed silently for everything to work out, so they could be a normal couple. These days she prayed to the universe as if it were a person. She called it different names: *God, Grandmother, Mother Earth, Gaia, Pachamama, Vallis, The*

Universal Intelligence Agency (UIA), and even *Glob* and *GForce,* her pet names for the nebulous energy she sensed, who stirred fate like the moon moved salt water. Today it was simply God, and all she asked was for Saman's protection.

When she finished praying, Thelma opened her eyes and looked at the clock again. Only ten minutes had passed. She sighed and glanced over at Saman's mother. The older woman sat still, with closed eyes. Was she also praying for Saman?

Come on time, hurry up.

Thelma visualized Saman. She imagined holding his hand, sitting beside his bed in the recovery room. She wanted to picture a successful transplant, but a different image crowded her inner vision — the spider from her mushroom trip; it haunted her. She couldn't shake it. *Was it a bad omen?*

Thelma shuddered. *Fuck off,* she thought. *Everything will be fine.*

Still, in the recess of her mind, the blood-covered spider crawled.

⁂

LIKE A FLICKERING CANDLE, Saman awoke. Darkness and pain welled in his gut. He tried to open his eyes, but his vision was blurry. Forcing air past his lips, he attempted to speak. Nothing moved. Saman's mind struggled, stuck in the dark realm of a half-over dream, his midriff an oozing wound.

Then a searing, scalding suffering pierced his abdomen. Hot racing pain, biting sensations, and the attack of a blade cut him. He could think and feel, but he couldn't speak or see. A cold knife raked through his skin. He tried to move every muscle in his body. He screamed in silence, trapped in blackness. He would do anything to escape this tormenting pain. Blood gurgled from his open stomach.

I'm frozen, he thought. *Am I paralyzed? I'm awake.*

No sound came from his lips. Walls and waves of pain radiated through his midsection and out to his limbs. The blackness oscillated with a yellow and blue fog. The ceiling of the room came in and out of focus. *The Pain.* The pain was too great. An electrical storm bolted through his body.

What was happening? *Am I awake? Is this a dream? I'm dying. I've woken up because I'm dead. This can't be.* No dream could contain this level of physical agony.

"Suction please," a man's voice.

I can hear you. I'm awake. He screamed inside his head.

Pain.

Beat.

Pain.

Music played in the background. He willed himself to focus on the notes, anything to escape the stabbing in his stomach.

What is that song? Am I going crazy? He was caught somewhere between alive and asleep.

Why am I awake?

The light dimmed; the shadow of a man loomed over him speaking garbled sounds.

Saman disassociated, separating his mind from his body. *Go away. Get out of here.*

He heard the music again. It was familiar. *That song, what was it?*

Tools burned his skin. Objects shifted his organs. He felt everything. Voices warped around the room.

You're killing me, he tried to scream. He imagined wiggling his toes. He begged his fingers to straighten. *Pain.*

Pain. Pain. Pain. Nothing happened but pain and the machines beeping faster and faster, the buzz of something electric, a tearing, a cutting.

He disconnected from his body again, to leave himself. The song still played in the background. He recognized the words now. The song was *Oyster Dreams* by *The Rock Farmers*.

> *My love, she's winding down.*
> *My love of life, it's underground.*
> *Let me experience this bliss,*
> *this fading oyster's dream,*
> *the pearl that I am.*

The lyrics were faint, but he could hear them. *I'm awake, and no one knows I'm awake.* The realization turned his pain to terror. Sucking noises drowned out the music. *Was he imagining things? Why would they play that song?*

He smelled burning hair, or was it plastic? He smelled metal too, or was it blood? Everything moved inside his stomach. Something snapped and gurgled, another broken piece of his gut. Liquid gushed and organs sloshed. Hands touched his body.

Overwhelmed by physical misery, he lost his grip on reality.

"His heartbeat is really erratic," a nurse said.

"He's not breathing," a woman's voice, louder, more urgent.

"He's in distress," a man.

The Pain. Only pain. I'm dying, Saman decided. The world slipped away. Then he died.

THELMA STOOD in front of the vending machine, debating on buying a *Lightning Shark*. She was trying to quit drinking energy drinks, but the idea of a pick-me-up was tempting. She fed a dollar into the slot and the *Lightning Shark* popped out. As she returned to her seat, the cool aluminum can in hand, Saman's surgeon entered the waiting area. Thelma stopped walking. *Please let there be no complications.*

"I'm happy to report that the transplant was a success," the doctor said, smiling. Thelma exhaled a sigh of relief. The doctor continued, "Rita and Saman are in the recovery room resting. You can see them soon."

Thelma shook the doctor's hand. "Thank you. Thank you so much."

The doctor nodded. "You're welcome. Saman had some erratic heart activity midway through the procedure, but we stabilized him. His body is accepting the new kidney."

"*Khoda ro shokr!*" Saman's mother said, raising her arms.

"Rita did great," the doctor added, "Absolutely no issues on her end. She should recover quickly."

"Praise *Allah*," Saman's mother said in her Persian accent. "I'll call the rest of the family."

Relief and joy filled Thelma's body. She relaxed. Finally, their marriage could really start. They'd take their honeymoon. *Thank you, universe.* She could already picture them wading into a Hawaiian waterfall, hand in hand.

TIME SUSPENDED. Saman remembered tubes. Needles. Air shot into his lungs. His throat burned. His stomach ached. He winced. His head turned. It actually moved. He opened his eyes. They really opened. He could see.

I'm alive, he realized. *It was over.* He blinked, stunned. *What had happened?*

A heavyset nurse with graying brown hair came to his side. "Ah, you're awake. You did great." She put her hand on his shoulder.

"Thelma," he choked out, "Thelma." Speaking sent splinters of discomfort down his raw throat.

The nurse leaned over him, concerned, "Are you in a lot of pain?"

"I was awake." He forced the words out, each syllable a struggle.

The nurse frowned and patted his shoulder. "You'll feel better soon."

He grimaced. He wanted to say more, but it hurt to make sounds.

The nurse checked his medical devices. "If the pain gets worse, press this button." She moved his hand to a small, square remote attached to the bed.

"I was awake." Saman's throat ached.

The nurse glanced at him. "Yes, you're awake now. The surgery was a success."

Did I imagine everything? He wondered, confused. No, it was impossible. Something had gone wrong. "Please," he asked again, "Can you get my wife?"

"She'll come in soon. Try to rest. I'll be right here if you need anything. You can suck on this." She placed a small, damp sponge between his cracked lips.

The nurse left Saman's field of vision. The sponge sunk into his dry tongue. The surgery should have been a blank spot in his memory, but he could remember long moments of terrible pain. He remembered trying to scream. He remembered the paralysis.

Sucking on what little liquid was in the sponge,

Saman's head pounded with unanswered questions. Pain splintered through his midsection. He pressed the morphine button the nurse had given him. His heart pounded. The surgery was over, so why did he still feel so afraid?

THELMA'S VOICE pierced his drugged haze, "Saman?"

Opening his eyes, his wife came into view beside his hospital bed with a soft smile and concern in her blue eyes.

"Thelma," he breathed.

"Babe, how do you feel?"

He reached for her hand. Tears threatened to form in the corner of his eyes, not from pain, but from relief. She was here. He was alive. He'd survived. "I love you."

"I love you, too." She touched his leg through the thin hospital sheet. "You did great."

"Rita? Is she okay? Have you seen her?" It no longer hurt to speak; the pain killers had finally numbed him.

Thelma nodded, "Yes, she's fine. She's with Juan."

Saman closed his eyes. He wanted to cry, but why? He felt exhausted, overwhelmed.

"Do you need anything?" Thelma asked. "Can you drink water?"

"Something terrible happened," he murmured, remembering.

Thelma leaned over, concerned. "No, babe, you did great. You're in the recovery room. Everything was fine."

"No. It was awful. I was awake."

She rubbed his leg. "Awake?"

"I woke up in the surgery." He shook his head, "I don't know what happened. Something went wrong."

"What?" Thelma leaned closer, "What did you say?"

"I woke up during the surgery. I felt everything, but I couldn't move." A tear slid out onto his cheek.

Thelma stared at him, confused, but he couldn't explain more now. He needed to sleep. He closed his eyes and sifted like sand back through the hourglass of his unconscious mind.

4

Thelma watched Saman sleep. Gone was the yellow tint the dialysis imparted on his skin. Only a day after the new kidney, and already he looked 100 times healthier. His physical body was recovering at least...

While Saman dozed, she tried to meditate, but her intuition was useless in this context of tubes and pills and paperwork. Exhaustion tugged at her. She'd barely slept since Saman's operation, her empathy for Saman made it hard to relax, given his tortured state.

The hospital staff moved around them like silent witnesses, afraid of saying the wrong things. As if on trial, they worded sentences with care, their eyes cast to the floor.

"That's highly unlikely," the head surgeon had said when Saman explained that he was conscious during part of the operation. A nurse suggested it was a dream, another doctor said a trauma or anxiety response. The anesthesiologist asserted that Saman's behavior was a normal reaction.

Thelma wasn't so sure. She'd never seen Saman so frustrated.

Someone knocked on the door, interrupting Thelma's thoughts. Saman stirred in bed.

A woman in an ill-fitted skirt suit entered the room. She held a folder. "I'm from the business office. I'd like to review some forms you signed prior to intake."

Thelma stood and whispered, "Saman is asleep."

"I'm awake now," Saman said, eyes open.

The lady continued, "These documents outline the risks of complications that you were made aware of before your operation."

Thelma's palms started to sweat. Saman had snapped at the last person from the business office.

"I know what I signed!" Saman shot back.

Thelma moved closer to the bed. "Babe, let's do this so we can go home."

"No, I will not. Not until someone here tells the truth." Saman folded his arms across his chest.

The woman eyed Thelma. "I'll leave the documents for your review. Please have your husband sign the first and last page."

"I'll be contacting malpractice lawyers," Saman said, "and, believe me, we will pursue a settlement."

The woman ignored him. "Well, I'll let you rest now."

"Thank you, sorry, we're all very tired," Thelma explained. The woman gave her a knowing look and left.

"Why are you siding with those assholes?" Saman said as soon as the door shut. "Don't apologize to them."

Thelma exhaled, "They're just doing their jobs."

Saman pursed his lips and shook his head, "It's like you don't believe me, either."

"Babe, that's not true. Of course, I believe you, but berating the staff won't help the situation."

Saman shook his head with disgust. "We need a lawyer."

Before she could respond, there was another knock on the door.

Thelma groaned inwardly, but said, "Come in."

A middle-aged woman with short brown hair and dressed in a navy-blue pants suit entered the room. "Hi, I'm Dr. Bronson."

Saman glared at her.

"I'm a clinical psychologist, and I'll be doing a patient evaluation," she continued.

"No, I already talked to the shrink," Saman said.

Thelma's eyes widened. She couldn't believe how rude Saman was behaving since the transplant, snapping at almost everyone they came into contact with. It was so unlike him that it was hard for her to process.

The psychologist nodded, "I understand you saw a psychiatrist, but I'm here to assess if you're ready to head home."

Saman scowled. "Thelma, please record this conversation on your phone."

Thelma froze. How could someone's personality shift so quickly?

"That isn't necessary," the doctor replied.

"I said record this," Saman turned to Thelma and raised his eyebrows, "or, if you won't, I will. Give me my phone."

Thelma didn't move. *Why couldn't Saman cooperate?*

The psychologist sat down in a nearby armchair, "I'd rather not be recorded."

"Yeah, and I'd rather not be cut open while I'm wide awake," Saman said. "I suppose you've come to tell me that I'm suffering from delusions caused by stress, that I'm imagining things, that I'm making everything up to get attention, that I wasn't awake, and that this is all normal?"

A disappointed expression passed over the doctor, then

she shook her head. "I'm afraid I don't understand. Why don't you explain the situation to me?"

"I've explained enough," Saman glowered, "I'm sure it's all right there in your fucking folder."

The psychologist blinked and then with a cold professionalism said, "The sooner you answer the questions, the sooner you can be on your way."

Thelma went to Saman's side and squeezed his hand, "Please, babe."

"Give me my phone."

Thelma hesitated, but then passed Saman his phone from the window sill where it had been plugged in and charging. *Anything to get this over with,* she thought.

Saman switched on the phone's camera and gritted his teeth. "Go ahead."

The therapist frowned and made a note on her clipboard, "Very well, this won't take too long."

Thelma sat at the foot end of Saman's bed, staring at her hands, folded on her lap, as the psychologist ran through a series of standard questions. Saman answered each with the shortest and rudest responses he could muster.

When the interview was over the psychologist said, "Anesthesia awareness is very rare, but it can cause post-traumatic stress disorder."

Saman glared at her. "No shit."

"You need to avoid stress and get plenty of rest," the doctor continued, "the more you can relax, the faster you'll feel better."

"He's been having nightmares and talking in his sleep," Thelma mentioned.

"You know what I think would help me heal?" Saman's eyes narrowed as he tossed out the words like rotten meat.

"What would help is if anyone here gave an actual fuck to admit they made a mistake." His voice rose and cracked, "I'm telling the truth. I woke up. I remember what people were saying. I heard them say my heartbeat was erratic. How could I have known that?" Saman shook his head. "But no one will admit they messed up." He raised his arms, "All they care about is not getting sued."

"I'm not saying you didn't wake up." The doctor made another note, "I'm recommending your release, but I'll refer you to an out-patient therapist, to help you adjust to post-surgery life, and you've been prescribed an anti-depressant, so keep taking that."

"Yep. Pass out more pills. Whatever," Saman said, shaking his head.

Thelma followed the psychologist into the hallway. "I'm so sorry. He's not usually like this. It's been a very stressful time."

The psychologist considered her words. "Listen, I'm sorry, I really am, but the medication will help. I know this must be difficult for you, and not what you were expecting, but he needs to stop dwelling on the surgery." The psychologist handed Thelma a business card, "This therapist specializes in men with PTSD."

Thelma nodded. "Thank you."

As the doctor walked away, tears slid down Thelma's cheeks. Between Saman's outbursts and her own lack of sleep, she wished she had a morphine button to push. Instead of returning to the hospital room, she stopped at a vending machine and bought another *Lightning Shark* energy drink, her second of the day. Then, she left the building.

Wandering down the sidewalk in the hot Miami sun,

Thelma found an empty bench under an old Florida oak tree and sat down. She'd look for a lawyer like Saman wanted, but first, she needed a break.

5

Four Months Later.

The early morning dawn washed Plantation, Florida with mauve and silver light. Saman drove into the *Hello Sunshine Morning Show*'s parking lot. He missed the old downtown station, with six recording studios, an open reception area, sleek glass walls and marble floors. Now, out in the suburbs, the office occupied one floor in a dingy yellow building and looked more like a dentist's office than a hip radio show. "Changes in the industry and raising real estate costs in South Florida" were the reasons the company's owner gave for the relocation.

Kayla's car was already in the front row, beside the handicap spot. *Some nerve*, Saman thought as he parked in the second row and pulled his keys out of the ignition. He never took that space. He always left it for José or Cynthia, the on-air personalities. He scowled, *GenZ — they have no respect for workplace hierarchies*.

The morning show would start in a few minutes. Saman trudged to the second-floor sound booth. José waived hello to him. Cynthia ignored him, staring at her cellphone instead.

Kayla waited next to his chair. "Hey," she mouthed, her bubble-gum colored lips parting to reveal perfect, straight white teeth. Her Russian heritage gave her a doll face, accentuated by the heavy makeup she wore. On her YouTube channel, she called herself Kay Dash, but her real name was Kayla Dashkevich. He might think she was hot if he didn't already hate her.

Saman cocked his head in a silent, nonchalant acknowledgment of her presence, then slid into his chair behind the audio controls. He disliked running the show with Kayla sitting so close. She was always twirling her hair or sucking on green smoothies through a bamboo straw. The station director wanted her to do Saman's job while he was on his honeymoon. *Fat chance she won't mess things up*, he thought, adjusting his headphones.

The show kicked off. Saman struggled to suppress his yawns. Ever since the transplant, he'd been plagued with nightmares. *I'll get more coffee after this*, he told himself. To keep himself alert, he focused on Jose's jokes. The two hosts took callers and cracked up over the latest south Florida crime-gossip. He glanced at Kayla. She was scrolling through pictures of herself on her phone. He rubbed his eyes. *Only an hour left*.

Finally, the show was over. Saman hit the auto-play on the commercials that would run between segments. They cleared into the hallways to make room for the next hosts.

"See you guys tomorrow," Cynthia waved goodbye. Kayla

disappeared to the bathroom. *No wonder*, Saman thought, *after that giant jar of algae she was drinking.*

"Great show," Saman said to José, "That bit about the stinky socks in the Children's Museum was hilarious."

"Ha! You liked that? Thanks, man," José pat his shoulder, "When do you leave again?"

"Next week," Saman replied.

José raised his eyebrows, "*YouTubey* will be so excited to fly solo again."

Saman grinned at José's nickname for Kayla. "Right. Between you and me, I can't wait for her internship to end."

"Oh yeah, man, I can tell. I think she can tell too. She acts all nervous around you."

Before Saman could respond, the next show's host came down the hallway.

"See you tomorrow," José said.

Saman went to the break room to make a fresh pot of coffee. While the black liquid brewed, he poured a glass of water and pulled out a palm-sized, plastic yellow pill case and popped two white capsules into his mouth, swallowed, then chased the kidney meds with Prozac, which was supposed to help with his PTSD symptoms, though he suspected it made him even more tired.

Coffee bubbled to the top of the pot, and he filled his giant thermos to the brim. There was a pile of administrative work on his to-do list and a meeting with Ron, the station manager. Steaming coffee in hand, he approached his office. As he got closer, a high-pitched voice chirped from behind the door. It sounded like a Disney princess, if the Disney Princess drank triple-espresso Pumpkin Spice Lattes and snorted Ritalin for breakfast.

"And guys, here's my desk. I work soooo early. I've already been here for like hours. Every morning I'm like

WHY? Why do I do this? But you guys know why! Because I love it! And if you want to get a job in radio, click the link below and watch my other video on how I got a job in radio!"

Saman paused outside the door, listening. *Got a job in radio? What a crock of shit; she was an intern.* She was probably showing her followers *his* desk and pretending it was hers. He resented every day that he still had to share an office with her.

"So, if you loved this tour, tap like and hit that subscribe button! And goodbye from the *Hello Morning Show*! Love you guys!"

He opened the door.

Kayla jumped from leaning on his desk. "Oh hey, I didn't realize you were here. I was recording my vlog."

"I heard." Saman maneuvered past her and sat down. Kayla wedged herself in between his desk and a shelf of equipment. She wore a short, skin-tight jean skirt and a baggy pink top that hung way off her shoulder on one side, with a black and white picture of an atomic bomb's mushroom cloud. Her bleach-blond hair emphasized thick, jet-black eyebrows and her necklace looked more like shoelaces than jewelry.

"Um," she said, "so, I was thinking, I could color code our task-list from Ron, so make all the quick tasks one color, all the longer tasks another color, and put them in categories and then tack them on the wall, too, so we don't miss anything again. What do you think?"

He switched on his computer, considering his response. How could he dismiss her idea, which sounded confusing and tiresome, while still sounding polite?

She repeated her question, "So, should I color code it? I think it would definitely help, and then I can remind you of stuff, so you don't forget anything. There's an app I use to track stuff. I can send reminders to your phone."

He blinked, "Remind me of stuff? Kayla, you aren't my secretary."

She looked down. "Well, I thought it might help, you know, after what happened with Cynthia last week."

Irritation boiled like water in Saman's gut. "Listen that kind of stuff happens sometimes. It's not a big deal." He swallowed, pausing the way his therapist had taught him to do when he felt frustrated.

"Sorry, just trying to help," Kayla said, shrugging.

Saman looked away. *Interns should be banned,* he thought. But instead, he said, "Okay, color code the to-do list, but first, load the spots for tomorrow, go over them, and make sure we've got all the files on the list. Double check the formats."

"Do you have any color preferences? Or any categories you want?"

He took a swig from his coffee thermos and sat it back down beside his keyboard. "Um, I'll think about it and please make a written plan with the color code so I can approve it first." *That'll stall her*, he thought, *then I won't approve the plan.*

"Okay, but shouldn't I pull together those supply receipts and make the spreadsheet Ron wanted?"

Fuck. He'd totally forgotten about the supply audit. Still, Kayla didn't need anymore reasons to play secretary. "No, I already started," He lied. "Just do what I asked, please."

"Alrighty, then," she twirled around in an exaggerated gesture on the backs of her high heels, like Dorothy trying to escape Oz. As she turned, her right arm connected with his coffee thermos and knocked it over. Hot coffee poured onto his keyboard. He shot up from his chair as the brown liquid flowed under his external hard drive and dripped off the edge of his desk.

"Jesus Christ, Kayla!" he exploded. "Watch what you're doing!" He frantically moved the external hard drive, as the coffee spread under his monitors and flowed onto the floor. "Get me some fucking paper towels, right now! You stupid child!" he yelled.

Kayla froze, staring at him with her mouth wide open.

"Paper towels!" Saman yelled again. "Go!"

"It was an accident," she exclaimed, scrunching her eyebrows, about to cry. She ran out of the room.

He tried to sop up the spill with printer paper. "Stupid fucking idiot," he mumbled under his breath, but as he attempted to contain the coffee, his chest tightened with anxiety. He'd gone too far, yelling at Kayla like that. He should've controlled himself. *Who knows what she'll tell Ron…?* Saman swallowed and tried to calm down. He'd apologize when she came back. That was all he could do.

On command, she opened the door and dropped a wad of paper towels onto his desk. "There you go," she said, her tone as friendly as an ice pick.

Spreading out the towels to soak up the remaining liquid, he turned to her, "Hey, Kayla, I'm so sorry, I shouldn't have gone off on you like that."

She crossed her arms.

"That was unprofessional," he added, studying her reaction. "Again, I'm sorry."

"Whatever," She pursed her lips, then sat down in front of her computer.

Fuck, Saman thought. The tension in the room was almost unbearable. He tried to focus, but his mind bounced from worry to worry. He imagined Kayla giving him the middle finger behind his back. College kids were really sensitive these days, he knew, and they weren't shy about speaking up.

After about ten minutes, Kayla swished past him, heels clicking on the floor.

Panic seized Saman as he watched her leave. *This wasn't good. Kayla might also tell Cynthia. That would be worse than Ron knowing.* Cynthia already wanted Ron to fire him. The station had paid to have a famous Miami rapper named Black Corleone come for an interview. During the show, Cynthia's mic had short-circuited. Saman didn't realized, so the audience heard long pauses in between the rapper's responses. The interview sounded so strange that it made the news and left Ron dealing with Black Corleone's irate manager and a PR fiasco. Saman had apologized profusely for his mistake, but Cynthia was still pissed.

The splattered coffee stained his pants like freckles. His computer chair was damp. He struggled to concentrate on his spreadsheet. Twenty minutes passed. *Had Kayla left the station? That was the best-case scenario. Maybe she would just quit.*

But an hour later, Kayla returned. "Ron wants to see you," she said with a sickly-sweet smile and narrowed eyes that left no room for doubt — *she'd told Ron everything.*

Saman stopped typing and stared at his computer. *Shit. I've really messed up now.*

6

⸻

Outside of Ron's closed door, Saman paused. How would he explain his behavior? *Should I blame it on the PTSD?* He wondered. Ron didn't have much sympathy for his health situation, at least not after his medical leave had run out. *Maybe deny it had happened?* It would be his word against hers, but would Ron believe Kayla had lied? Probably not. All he could do was to tell the truth, that she drove him nuts, that she'd spilled coffee everywhere and he'd exploded; anyone would have done the same. He took another deep breath and knocked on the door.

"Come in," Ron called.

Saman complied. The station's HR officer sat in a chair opposite Ron.

Crap. He tried to act like everything was normal. "Kayla said you wanted to see me?"

"Have a seat," Ron gestured, raising his eyebrows, which caused the heavy wrinkles on his forehead to furrow in rows of thick, Florida-sunned skin.

Sweat collected in droplets under Saman's armpits as he

lowered himself into the chair. "I'm almost done with the supply audit. I only need about thirty more minutes."

"Saman, I'm not going to sugarcoat this." Ron leaned forward, elbows on the desk. "You've been a valuable employee here, but I'm afraid you're causing significant conflicts with other staff, and I have to let you go. Sandy has paperwork for you to sign, and we'd like you to clear out your desk and head home when this meeting ends."

Saman blinked. *What? Leave the station? Was he getting fired? Over this? Over Kayla? What had Kayla said?* He didn't know what to say. *How could Ron do this?* He'd been here longer than Kayla and Cynthia combined.

Sandy, the HR lady handed him the forms and a pen. "Please read through this and initial that you've read each page. Then sign where indicated."

In a state of shock, Saman took the pages from her, and held them on his lap. All the times he had contemplated quitting the station, or leaving to go back to University, he'd never imagined it would end like this.

He made eye contact with Ron, "Kayla spilled coffee all over all my equipment; anyone would be upset, and if this is about the thing with Cynthia's mic — I assure you, that will never happen again."

"Saman, I don't want to get into the weeds on this. I've made my decision. If you need a reference, I'll give you one, but it's time to move on." Ron picked up a fist-sized, foam football from off his desk and squeezed it. "Think of this as a new start."

Clenching the papers, rage overwhelmed Saman and a flurry of words tumbled out of his snarling lips. "I just bought a house and I'm supposed to be taking my wife on our honeymoon. I'm registered for night classes at Nova. I can't afford to be unemployed right now. This is not how you treat valuable employees." He wanted to scream and possibly cry or punch Ron in the face, maybe all three at the same time. Ron glanced at Sandy, who offered a meek smile.

"Is there any way you could rethink this? I'll do HR training or whatever you want me to do. I'm really sorry for my behavior. It's been a tough few months, you know." Saman tried to calm his tone.

"I'm so sorry, Saman," Ron said. "Our decision is final."

Saman's jaw locked. He opened his mouth to speak, but instead, closed it and left. *What was the point?* The heat of shame burned his cheeks as he exited the building. What would he tell Thelma? What job could he get fast enough for them to keep up their mortgage payments?

In his car, Saman hit the steering wheel and screamed, "Fuck!" He peeled out of the station at high speed and drove to a nearby Target Department Store. Parking in a far corner, he flicked open the glove box and took out his other pill jar, the one he kept to himself, the one he hid.

The white pill tasted like bleach as he choked it down dry. Resting his forehead on the steering wheel of his car, he squeezed both of his forearms with his opposing hands, digging in so deep that his skin broke. Blood oozed under his fingernails, like tiny red smiles without teeth. Holding himself, he waited for relief, for his body to digest the pain medication, to turn it from chemical powder to sweet peace.

FRIED EGGS JIGGLED on the plate as Thelma put breakfast in front of Saman.

"Do you want salt and pepper?" she asked.

He nodded, "Thanks, my love."

Thelma went back into the kitchen.

Saman stared at the eggs. Nothing looked good to him anymore. The doctors had said he'd gain weight after the kidney transplant, but he was still underweight for his height. Out the window, the sun was shining, at least for now. It had been raining a lot lately. He missed the *Hello Sunshine Morning Show*. Without a job, and with no dialysis appointments, his sense of time dragged into a shapeless, long day. He watched television, programmed music on his computer, recorded nature sounds, or played video games. Occasionally, he drove to the pet store to get cat food for StanGetz.

Yawning, he turned his fork sideways and cut into the egg. Bright yellow liquid squirted onto the plate. The yolk spread on the white ceramic. His mind wandered.

"Are you okay?" Thelma came back from the kitchen, holding her coffee mug.

He raised his eyes. "Yeah, I'm not that hungry, sorry."

Thelma put her coffee down on the table. In a blue linen sundress, she embraced him, cradling his head against her stomach, standing next to his chair. "You should eat."

He hugged her hips. "I will."

She tilted his face up and kissed him.

He gazed at her, "I don't know if we should take this trip. Do we really want to spend money right now?"

Thelma stepped back, "I think we need this vacation more than ever."

He shook his head, "We could postpone, go after I find another job."

"Babe, you can find a job when we get back, or you can switch from the evening program and go full time to school. Plus, if you got a new job now, you wouldn't have any time off." She smiled and ruffled her hands through his hair. "This is actually the perfect time to go."

Saman sighed. His chest felt hollow. He hadn't yet confessed to Thelma that he'd unenrolled himself from University in a self-destructive rage after being fired. At least he'd been able to get a refund. He rubbed his eyes. "I don't know."

"Plus, if you're going to have panic attacks, you may as well have them in Hawaii," Thelma grinned.

Maybe she's right, he thought. Still, the idea of traveling so far made him nervous, though he couldn't really explain why.

Thelma squeezed his shoulders. "Wait till we're snorkeling and watching the hula dancers."

He tried to smile, "Hula dancers — yes, snorkeling — no. You realize sharks live in the ocean, right?"

Thelma scoffed, "People snorkel all the time. A shark could eat us here. I'd love to scuba dive with the giant manta rays."

"That doesn't sound safe."

She smiled, "It'll be a great change of scenery."

He nodded. *Even better than a change of scenery would be if the settlement money from the hospital comes through.* He forced a smile, "You're probably right,"

"Of course, I'm right."

"Maybe, I'll love it so much that I won't want to leave."

"Your mother will kill me if I don't bring you back."

"I'll tell her to complain to Allah, since it will be his will," Saman joked.

Thelma impersonated Saman's mother's Persian accent, *"Inshallah, Inshallah."*

Saman laughed. "Okay, that's creepy."

"Speaking of your mom, when are you going to drop off StanGetz? You should probably do it the day before. We leave so early."

"Enough about my mother." Saman pulled Thelma in closer and inched his hand up her dress.

"Mmm," she said and traced the edge of his right ear with her finger.

He squeezed her breast with one hand and cupped the other hand around her buttocks. Then moved to the front of her body and rubbed between her legs. *At least my dick still works,* he thought.

"Hey," she pulled back, "We don't have time, remember today is Maria's birthday party."

"We've got time." He rubbed her crotch again.

"Naughty, naughty," Thelma said, grinning as she climbed onto his lap, straddling him at the kitchen table.

He wrapped his arms around her firm bottom and pressed her into his erection. "That's more like it."

She kissed him and he rocked her against his jeans, rubbing her body on his crotch.

"Let's go in the bedroom," she whispered.

"No, right here."

She leaned back and pulled out his erect cock.

He gazed at her with nothing but love in his heart. He admired almost everything about her, the calm way she carried herself, her work ethic, and her constant drive to create meaningful art, to help other people. *What would I do without her?* He wondered, as she guided him to the soft, pink entrance between her thighs.

DRIVING INTO THE PLANNED COMMUNITY, with its brand-new matching builder homes, and manicured lawns, Saman wondered what the suburban neighbors would think if they knew Maria and her husband were total psychonauts, psychedelic explorers, who drank *ayahuasca*, ate *peyote*, and hosted *wachuma* cactus-medicine ceremonies almost every weekend? He chuckled at the thought. From the outside, Maria looked like anyone's *abuela* — like a Colombian grandma, which she also was. Her *pandebono,* a soft bread filled with cheese, was Saman's favorite.

Children raced across Maria's yard, playing tag and laughing. Saman and Thelma held hands as they walked into the party. Balloons and streamers hung from the safety fence around the swimming pool. Extended family, kids, and grandkids, plus all the people who regularly attended the medicine circles, filled the Mediterranean-style house. Holding two bouquets of sunflowers, daisies, and lilies, one for Maria and one for Rita, Saman spotted Rita by a picnic table, seated next to her boyfriend. She was eating from a plate of shredded pork, plantains, and corn on the cob. He caught her eye and waived. She bounded over, leaving the hot food.

"Young man! How are you!" Rita hugged him, then embraced and kissed Thelma on the cheeks. "All my favorite children are here!" she exclaimed.

"Ah, I didn't mean to interrupt your lunch," Saman said, returning her embrace.

"Nonsense," Rita grinned, "I shouldn't eat that anyway!"

"Ahh, you look great." Thelma said.

Rita beamed, "I didn't know if you guys were coming or if you'd be too busy getting ready for Hawaii."

"We leave next week," Thelma said, "and we couldn't miss this!"

Maria joined the group. "My dears, so glad you came!" She hugged Thelma and Saman.

"Happy birthday!" Thelma gushed.

"Sixty years young right here!" She pointed to herself,

then she swished her skirt and winked. "But how are you guys doing?"

Saman shrugged, "Same old, same old."

"And how's the radio station?" Maria asked. "You know I listen every morning!"

Saman's words caught in his throat, then he muttered, "Good, good," and looked away, ashamed to be lying to Maria. *Why was he lying?* He hadn't told anyone besides Thelma about being fired. Admitting he no longer worked at the station was hard to accept, much less say out loud.

Thelma shot him a disappointed look. "We're very excited to have a break, looking forward to the honeymoon."

"Oh yes," Rita said, "I see your social media and you are so busy, with all the photoshoots, and creating such amazing artwork."

It was true, Saman thought, Thelma was in high demand for photoshoots. If they were living in New York she'd probably be taking pictures for big magazines by now.

"Ah, thank you," Thelma said, blushing.

"You two ladies come and help me bring out the salads and the fruit." Maria motioned for Rita and Thelma to join her in the house.

Saman wandered over to the BBQ grill, where Maria's husband was grilling meat, but he was talking in Spanish to another man. Saman sat down at a small table and looked around. He did not recognize anyone else in the backyard. Maria's son spotted him and came over with a beer. He was a short and round man who looked like Maria, always with a mischievous grin on his face.

"Thanks," Saman said.

"You're the one who had the organ transplant, right?"

"That's me," Saman said.

"Amazing, man, amazing. I'm Joe, Maria's son."

"Saman." He shook Joe's hand. "We met before, but it's been a while."

"Right, you're the one who met your wife at my mom's ceremony, right? I saw pictures from your wedding. It looked great."

Saman nodded. "Yeah, that's us. We're actually about to take our honeymoon."

"Oh, amazing. Where are you going?"

"Hawaii," Saman smiled.

Joe threw up his hands in exaggerated shock. "Dios mío, man, wow wow wow wow wow! Hawaii? I'm jealous."

Saman chuckled. Maria's son talked exactly like her.

"Yep, we're pretty excited."

Joe took a swig of beer, "I have a friend in Hawaii. You should meet him. I can connect you guys. You will love him." Joe turned and yelled towards his mom who was coming out of the house trailed by a stream of women all carrying disposable aluminum trays full of more food.

"Eh, Mamá, over here." He waved his hand.

Maria came, holding a tray of shredded pork. "My son, what do you want? Can't you see I'm busy?" she teased Joe.

"Hey, they have to meet Bāne Kama," Joe said to his mother.

Maria made an 'o' shape with her lips. "Ah-hah, you're right." Maria nodded, "Yes, yes. I can't believe I forgot to tell you. He lived here, but he moved to Hawaii. He hosted the best ceremonies. The best! You'll love him. And his medicine is powerful. He's a wild man. You must go and see him while you're there. He has a beautiful place. I've seen pictures."

"What kind of ceremonies?" Thelma came to stand beside him, sipping lemonade.

"All kinds, the best kinds, children, grandfather, grandmother, all of them." Maria said. Children was code for mushrooms, grandfather for wachuma, and grandmother for ayahuasca. "Listen," Maria continued, "I'll tell him about you and give you his number. Before you leave, text him and arrange a visit." She turned to Thelma, "Maybe you can even catch a ceremony. And you — with your special gifts, you must meet him."

"My gifts are more like curses these days, but yes, we'd love to meet any friend of yours. Which island is he on?"

"Nonsense. Don't say that! Never take your visions for granted. Many try for years to reach a level of sight that comes so easily to you. But which island? I don't know." Maria looked at Joe.

Joe shrugged, "The big one, I think? The one called Hawaii?"

Thelma nodded, "We're going to that island and also to Oahu." She glanced at Saman.

"Yes, of course, please, connect us," Saman agreed.

"I'm so jealous," Maria said, "I'm coming next time!" Then she bounced away like a balloon.

Joe wandered off in search of another beer, and Thelma, Rita, and Saman got plates of food and found a table. Maria's daughter struck a dinner bell. Saman winced. Loud sounds really bothered him lately, as if his ears had increased their sensitivity.

Maria's daughter rang the bell again. His body tensed. *Stay calm,* Saman thought.

"Bienvenidos todos!" Maria's daughter shouted. The kids ignored her, still squealing and doing cannonballs into the swimming pool. She struck the bell again, even louder. Saman gripped his glass bottle of beer. His therapist had told him to recite the alphabet whenever he felt like a panic attack might start, but it never helped. Instead, he played jazz songs in his head. He ran the tracks on repeat, trying to distract himself from the unwanted feelings that buzzed in his brain like angry wasps.

"Eh!" Maria's daughter shouted at the kids, "Zip it!" She made a motion with her hand of heads getting cut off and they quieted down. "Okay, everyone, let's wish my mother a happy birthday!" She removed a cloth to reveal a large layer-cake, stacked four-stories high and covered in yellow fondant. Maria's son lit big blue "60th" candles, surrounded by sparklers on top of the cake, and the crowd sang, "Happy birthday, happy birthday to you," in English, then in Spanish.

Saman shifted in his seat, filled with anxiety. *What is wrong with me?* The sounds of his own surgery returned to him — the electric cutting, flesh being pulled apart, cracking and beeping. He covered one ear with his hand.

Thelma glanced at him with a concerned expression and put her palm on his thigh, but all he felt was his own internal pain. Logically, he knew the surgery would never happen again, it wasn't stuck inside him, but like a child imagining a monster in the closet, it still scared him.

Sparklers on top of the cake popped and sprung yellow flecks of light. The party guests cheered louder and clapped as Maria blew out the candles. Joe held a knife with a long silver blade. It glinted in the sunshine. Saman's stomach churned. His heart pounded. The cacophony of people and kids closed in around him. He couldn't stay at the table. Joe plunged the knife into the cake, revealing a devil's-food red center.

As the blade slid out, Saman, overwhelmed with anxiety, stood and hurried inside the house. Bolting to the bathroom, he locked the door and sucked in ragged gasps of air, to steady himself. Then he dug into his pocket and removed a round pill. Lunging towards the sink, he swallowed it with tap water. Visions of blood and needles, scalpels and pain replaced the jazz music in his mind. He ran the water, flushed the toilet, stuffed a bathroom hand towel into his mouth, bit down, and screamed into the fabric.

THELMA DROPPED her purse on the kitchen counter. Things hadn't gone well at Maria's. Since losing his job, Saman's panic attacks were only getting more intense and more frequent. She sighed. *Maybe he was right, maybe they shouldn't go to Hawaii? Would a trip help? Or make Saman worse?*

She heard her husband switch on the TV and the Xbox. *Was texting this Bāne Kama person a good idea?*

"Fuck!" Saman shouted from the living room.

Thelma filled a glass with water. He was yelling at his video games again. *Maybe a ceremony is exactly what Saman needs...* She missed the rituals and the larger ceremonies. Before the transplant, she'd sat with the outdoor group for their various journeys every month, sometimes taking ayahuasca, and sometimes using mushrooms or wachuma, the cactus medicine, but now between Saman's health situation, her working more, and all the rain, she hadn't gone in months.

Wanting to escape the sounds of Saman's violent video games, she walked out into the sunny oasis of their backyard. Sitting in her favorite outdoor chair, she gazed at the old Florida oak tree that loomed taller than their house by their perimeter fence. Under the tree, a creature moved in the grass. It was a bright green iguana, the size of a small crocodile, sunning itself at the base of the tall tree. *Damn*, Thelma thought, *I wish I had my camera*. The creature was enormous and ancient looking, with a tail longer than its body, and scales so green that it glowed neon in the grass. It was possibly the biggest iguana she'd ever seen.

I need to show this to Saman. She slowly reached for her cell phone to take a photo. The green iguanas were an invasive species, and some people shot them with pellet guns, but Thelma thought they were beautiful and exotic, like shrunken dinosaurs.

As she raised her cellphone to take the picture, the iguana turned its head. She froze, but it was too late. The lizard scrambled for the oak tree at high speed, running elevated on its hind legs, vanishing into the tree's branches before she could catch a shot.

Dang, Thelma thought. In her haste to capture the iguana's image, she'd dropped the piece of paper Maria had given her. She picked it up and unfolded it. Below Bāne Kama's name and phone number, Maria had written something in small, cursive letters. Thelma peered at the words, trying to decipher Maria's writing.

It read:

> *"A long path requires many short steps.*
> *This is one step. Text him today.*
> *Why? Because I said so."*

Thelma grinned. *Okay Maria, if you insist.*

7

Loading StanGetz into his crate always riled the long-haired, gray cat.

"Meow," StanGetz pleaded.

"Shhh, shh," Saman said and passed some cat treats through the opening of the carry case. "Just going to Grandma's." He wished his mom would come to their house to feed StanGetz while they were in Hawaii. He preferred to leave the cat at home, but his mother drove less these days and complained that he had moved too far away. She didn't like the highway or the long, busy road that connected her in north Pompano to Saman in southwest Fort Lauderdale.

As he pulled into the parking lot of his mother's building, he noticed his sister Yalda's mini-van in one of the visitor spots. His mother had moved to the condo, occupied mostly by senior citizens and snowbirds, four years ago, complaining that their childhood home was too much for her to handle without his father.

"Merrrrow," StanGetz emoted more urgently as the car stopped.

"Yes, we're here," Saman said to the cat.

Drab, beige tiles and worn carpet covered the lobby. The damp smell of mildew complemented the early 90s aesthetic. As he lugged StanGetz and a suitcase packed with his food and litter box, Saman wished his mother had never moved into the old building. She deserved better, and surely with the damp air there was mold. No wonder she was always coughing. He sighed and made a mental note to talk to Yalda about trying to get her a HEPA filter, at least for her bedroom.

As he approached his mother's door, the smell of fresh bread, sumac, and saffron masked the old carpet's odor.

"Ahh, *salam azize delam. Ghorboonet beram!*" his mother exclaimed as he walked inside. It meant, "Hello, dearest to my heart. May I be sacrificed for you."

Saman grinned at the theatrics of the greeting, though his mom had lived in the United States more than half her life, she never lost her flair for the dramatics of the Persian language. In the condo's small kitchen, she chopped fresh herbs for *Sabzi Khordan,* a traditional Persian appetizer with feta cheese, walnuts, radishes, basil and mint. Two cooking pots simmered on the stove.

"Smells great in here," Saman said as he lowered Stan-Getz's carrier and opened the hatch for the cat to escape. The grey feline inched out of confinement and like a baby jaguar crouched and surveyed the apartment. "You didn't have to cook all this."

"Nonsense. You need to eat. I need to eat. Yalda needs to eat. So, we eat together." His mother opened the lid to a pot, venting a puff of savory steam. She stirred the contents with a wooden spoon.

"Where is Yalda? I saw her car outside."

His mother gestured to the bedroom. "Changing Suri's diaper."

"That kid is still in diapers?"

His mother raised her eyebrows. "Not my business, not my business, I tell myself." She shook her head with disapproval.

Saman reached for a piece of feta cheese.

"Hey, hey," his mom said, "wait for everyone. Where is Thelma anyway?"

"She's doing a portrait shoot."

"On a Saturday?" His mother shook her head, "What kind of home do you have if your wife is working every day. No wonder your house is a mess."

"Our house isn't a mess," Saman scowled, apparently it was also his day to get berated.

Yalda emerged from the bedroom with Suri trailing behind her, thumb in mouth.

"I hope you wrapped up that diaper before you put it in the trash," Saman's mother said.

"Of course." Yalda rolled her eyes, then hugged Saman, "How are you?"

"I'm fine. Hi, Suri," Saman waived at the child. "She's getting big."

"Too big for diapers, that's for sure," his mother added in Farsi.

Yalda sat at the small, round dining table by the kitchen. In the tiny, open-concept apartment, the kitchen, dining room and living room all flowed together in a bowling alley shape. Suri toddled behind her, then spotted StanGetz and made a beeline for the cat's tail.

"Hey," Saman lunged for her. "Never touch a cat's tail. It will get angry and scratch you."

Suri froze then scurried away, climbing into her mother's lap, thumb back in mouth.

Yalda wrapped her arms around the child.

"You baby her too much."

Yalda ignored their mother's comment and turned to Saman. "I bumped into your coworker the other day, at the bank."

Saman stiffened. "Oh yeah?" he tried to sound nonchalant.

"Yeah, Cynthia. I recognized her right away, though of course she didn't know who I was."

Fucking Cynthia, of all people, Saman thought. His heart rate increased. Hopefully Yalda hadn't spoken to her.

"So, I introduced myself."

"She's not the friendliest person," Saman muttered.

Yalda set Suri on the floor and the girl wandered to the toy box Saman's mother kept in the apartment for her grandkids.

Saman's mother leaned over the counter to listen.

"Well, it was interesting," Yalda said, a sly smile spreading across her face.

Saman's eyes narrowed.

"Because I introduced myself, and said she worked with my brother and she was like, oh who is your brother? And I said you, and she said, no, you don't work there anymore." Yalda cocked her head to the side, waiting for his response.

"What?" Saman's mother said.

Saman clenched his jaw. *Why the hell was Yalda bringing this up in front of his mother?*

"And I thought, huh, that's weird," Yalda said.

"You quit the radio station?" Saman's mother asked with disbelief in her voice.

"She actually said you didn't quit," Yalda replied, "You got fired for yelling at your intern."

What the fuck? Saman glared at Yalda. How dare Cynthia blab about his personal business to his sister.

"Is that true, Saman?" His mother stepped around the counter to the table. "You got fired?"

Saman fixed his eyes on Yalda. "I didn't get fired," he lied. "I got fed up with my intern, but I didn't get fired. I quit. I was ready to move on."

"Why would you quit?" His mother burst out. "You buy a house and then quit your job? What are you thinking? You think money grows on trees? Now your poor wife is working on a Saturday! What's wrong with you?"

Anger rumbled through Saman's body. He could feel his blood pressure rising. "I'll find another job when I get back from Hawaii."

"What kind of man quits his job right after getting married. You stay home all day while your wife works? How long has this been going on? I raised you better than this." His mom interjected sharply in Farsi. "Your father would be disappointed in you."

"Don't bring my father into this," Saman snapped.

"Well, he would be. He worked himself to death for you to have a better future and you throw away a good job? How will you pay for your house? I told you that house was too big."

Saman fumed. He didn't know what to say. "Worry about your own bills, and I'll worry about mine," was all he could manage. Inside his anger bubbled like one of his mother's pots on the stove. He hated being confronted and criticized, and he hated having to explain himself.

"Don't tell me you quit to go study that eco-whatever-it-is sound stuff?" His mother's eyes widened. "Tell me you didn't leave your job to listen to the birds chirp!"

"Bioacoustics. And I was not studying birds chirping!" His voice amplified its volume. He was yelling. *Fuck this situation,* he thought.

"Okay, trees talking. Even worse. That will only cost you more money and leads to no job."

"You're wrong. It's an emerging field. You don't understand because you can't see outside your own narrow little reality." He exploded; his face full of heat. "And you know what, I'm not hungry, and I've got a lot to do before we leave." He pointed to the bags he'd brought of his cat's things, "All of StanGetz's stuff is here, his food and his litter box, everything you need. Take good care of my cat." He headed for the door.

"Saman, come on. Lunch is almost ready. We didn't mean to upset you."

"Bye," Yalda said with a smug tone intended to convey her disapproval.

He ignored the women and left.

Navigating his sedan down Las Olas, a slow-paced tourist trap of ritzy boutiques and high-end restaurants, Saman fumed about Yalda's encounter with Cynthia. *Why had she repeated that to his mother without talking to him first? What a bitch Yalda could be sometimes*, Saman thought, gripping the steering wheel. Angry and distracted, he slammed his breaks to avoid hitting a group of young tourists meandering across the intersection.

Instead of going home, he decided to restock his drug supply. His old friend Reed lived off the main drag, on a narrow street, lined with tall Florida oak trees. Most of the roads were one way and you could get lost in the neighbor-hood. Passing sparkling blue canals with mega yachts, Saman pulled into Reed's driveway. His friend had inherited the large waterfront estate from a wealthy aunt who had no children of her own.

Saman rang the doorbell of the two story, modern cement house. A skinny girl, in her early twenties, with stringy blond hair, short shorts, and a tight pink tank top answered the door.

"Hey," Saman said.

"Hi. You here for Reed?"

"Yes." He followed the girl inside. The living room had white marble floors and massive windows that looked out onto the swimming pool in the backyard. The canal peaked through thick bushes and palm trees. A couple girls and guys hung out on the patio under shade sails, drinking cock-tails and lounging on outdoor sofas. Two girls and a tan, muscular man were also in the water, all topless and making out with each other. Two women with cameras on tripods filmed the scene from different angles. Saman tried not to stare.

"Saman!" Reed paused his video game, *Terror Hunters*, and got off the couch to hug Saman. He wore white and pink, flowered board shorts and a red satin robe with a giant "R" embroidered on the back in gold thread. His long, straw-berry blond hair hung to his shoulders in waves, and his pale skin stretched taught over a skinny, tattoo-covered chest.

"Hey, don't get up on my account," Saman plopped onto the couch.

"You check out the action outside?" Reed asked, tossing Saman a second video game controller.

"How could I miss it?" Out the window, the guy in the

pool was now sucking on the breasts of his cast mate, while the other porn actress massaged his muscular shoulders.

"They've been shooting for like a week straight, probably twenty pornos a day." Reed said.

Saman shook his head. "All the same guy?"

"Nah, different people. The girls have been so smoking hot, it's ridiculous." He gestured to a glass vaporizer on the coffee table. "You want to hit this?"

"Sure." Saman pulled out a pack of wet wipes from his back pocket and cleaned the mouthpiece of the pipe.

The skinny girl in the shorts stared at him, puzzled, from the sofa. Saman didn't care or explain why he was sterilizing the vaporizer. He couldn't be too careful about other people's germs. On the immunosuppressant medication he had to take for the new kidney, any kind of flu or serious cold could send him to the hospital. Lighting the vaporizer, he inhaled deeply and filled his lungs with a dense cloud of marijuana.

"Hey, easy there Jihadi, that's some serious shard." Reed grinned, referencing an old high-school nickname he'd given Saman as a joke.

Saman burst out laughing, coughing as smoke came out of his mouth. Reed laughed too, and the girl giggled. He'd hated being called Jihadi in high school, but, now, already blazed from the quick-acting vapor, it was hilarious.

"Trust me, I just visited my mom; shard is what I need." He drew again on the mouthpiece and blew out another puff of air.

"Remember when your mom found us in the basement with Krista Larson and flipped?" Reed laughed.

Saman chuckled, "I bet she's still pissed about it."

The weed kicked in even stronger, and the porn outside the window turned into a slow-motion movie. It was hard to look away. The male actor now had the two women on the side of the pool, penetrating one from behind while the other stroked his hanging ball-sack and fingered herself. Would Thelma be upset if she knew he was watching this? *Probably not*, he thought. *She'd think it was interesting. She was cool like that.* Picking up the video game controller, he said, "I'm going to Hawaii tomorrow."

"Oh, sweet, man." Reed shot cars in his video game while he spoke, "You want to re-load your supply before you go?" he asked. "Or wait, they got that Maui-Wowi out there. That shit is supposed to be the dankest."

"Yeah, I don't think I'll get any weed, but do you have any of the pills I like?"

Reed raised his eyebrows, "You should be careful with that stuff."

Saman pursed his lips, irritated by the comment, "It's to sleep on the plane. It's a really long flight."

"Okay man, I'm just saying." He leaned forward and yelled toward his kitchen, "Jucy!"

Saman looked at him, puzzled. "Jucy?"

Reed grinned, "Wait for it."

A caramel-skinned, beautiful woman with long, black hair emerged from the kitchen wearing a sheer, white dress that barely covered her large breasts. Saman gaped at her. *Where did Reed find these women?*

"This is my new assistant, Jucy," Reed said, winking at Saman. "She helps manage my clients."

"Yes, sir?" Jucy said.

"Please bring my medicine bag."

"Of course," Jucy went to fetch Reed's drugs.

"Interesting name," Saman said.

"It's short for Jucelene. She's Brazilian. And when I say

Brazilian, I mean *everywhere*." Reed grinned and raised his eyebrows up and down for emphasis.

Saman laughed. "I don't know how you manage yourself around all these beautiful women."

"It's a special gift I have. I love them and they love me."

Jucy returned holding a black, leather bag, the kind a businessman might carry on an airplane. Saman tried not to look at her nipples, visible through her dress.

"Thanks, sweetie," Reed said.

"No problem. I'm making lunch," she replied.

"Great, great."

She left them alone.

The white girl on the sofa with the long legs blew a bubble with pink gum. It popped and she sucked it back into her mouth.

"Dude," Saman said, "your life is like a movie."

Reed tossed him a prescription pill container. "I try. There you go. $150."

"Any chance I could get two?" Saman asked.

"That's a lot of sleeping on planes." Reed cocked his head, "How many planes you taking?"

"Figured I may as well stock up."

"That's the only one I have. Those aren't easy to get now. The government's locking it down, too many addicts in the news."

"I know, my doctor told me to take Advil, as if that will work after taking this."

"You in pain still from the surgery?"

"Sometimes."

"Oh man, that sucks, but try CBD. That's better for you. Get those prescription frog gummies. Those are tasty."

"Maybe," Saman said.

"Hey, you guys want some molly for the honeymoon? I got some really pure stuff."

Saman shook his head, "Thelma isn't into that. It makes her jaw hurt."

"Fair enough."

Saman stared at the prescription bottle. Guilt mixed with his marijuana high. *I'll quit in Hawaii,* he thought as he put the oxycodone in his pocket.

The two friends lapsed into silence, shooting bad guys on the TV while strangers fucked outside.

8

W aves rocked Saman's boat. The starry sky above twinkled like a thousand eyes.

"Saman, don't do that," Yalda snapped, holding little Suri in her arms. "You'll tip us over." The child sucked her thumb on her mother's lap. He stopped paddling the long, wooden outrigger canoe.

Something jolted them from underwater. *Why are we doing this at night?* he wondered, steering into an ocean wave. The boat tilted towards the black water.

"Saman," Yalda shouted, "Stop!"

"It's not me." He dragged the edge of his paddle in the water, to slow them down. Again, he felt a bump from below.

"What was that?!" his sister screamed. "Saman, please, we have to go back."

He tried to steady the canoe, but Suri let out a blood-curdling scream. An old woman in a cloak, with long white hair clutched Suri and cackled as the child struggled in the crone's grip.

"Suri!" Saman shouted and lurched forward to grab his

niece, but as he did the boat rolled over, swallowed by the sea. Water filled Saman's mouth and lungs. He opened his eyes and saw nothing. He heard a voice.

"Saman, wake up." Thelma said.

Hands pushed his shoulder from side to side. As if floating to the surface, his consciousness emerged and returned him to his waking life.

"What time is it?" he murmured, rolling over onto his back.

"You slept through the alarm," Thelma said, standing beside the bed with her hands on her hips. "Get dressed. We need to leave for the airport."

"I had a terrible dream."

"You can tell me about it later. I'm calling the Uber."

He dragged himself to the bathroom. He remembered his sister's horror-filled expression as she lifted off the boat with Suri. *Why had he dreamed such an awful thing?*

"Saman, come on, the driver is here!" Thelma shouted from the front door.

"I'm coming," he slid on his jeans, his head foggy. *Why had they chosen such an early flight?* It was going to be a long day.

"Let's go." Thelma passed him an insulated water bottle.

In a daze, he followed her outside.

As the driver drove to the highway, Saman felt carsick. *I should have ridden in the front,* he thought. Opening the water, he took a swig, hoping it would calm his stomach. As he swallowed, his morning muscle memory kicked in. *Shit. I forgot my pills.* He glanced at the car's radio display. *If we turned around now, maybe we could still make it.*

"Sorry," he said in a firm voice to the driver, "Can you go back to our house? I forgot something."

"Are you serious?" Anger bubbled in Thelma's blue eyes. "We'll miss our flight."

The driver hesitated. "So, should I go back?"

"Yes." Saman said, "I'm so sorry, I forgot my medication."

"Are you kidding me?" Thelma said, "Why didn't you put it in your bag last night?"

Saman's head swam. She was right, but he'd left the pills in yesterday's pants' pocket. "Sorry, I can't leave without them."

They lurched back toward the house. Thelma pursed her lips, eyes on the road.

Running inside, Saman grabbed the prescription pills and stuffed them into his pocket.

AFTER A RACE back to the airport, they jumped out of the Uber and ran to the ticket counter, dragging their suitcases.

"You're lucky," the airline attendant said as she scanned their tickets. "Two more minutes and you would have missed the check-in cutoff."

Saman, out of breath, hoisted their bags onto the conveyor belt.

When they finally were seated on the plane, he exhaled. This was not a good start for their honeymoon. He touched Thelma's knee. "Hey, I'm sorry about this morning."

She sighed, "It's fine. I'm going to sleep."

"Okay, me too."

"Don't forget to take your pills," she said, making the face she'd use to scold a child.

"I won't."

Thelma put on her headphones and an eye mask.

He reached for his book bag, then realized he'd left his water bottle in the Uber. *Fuck, Thelma wouldn't like that at all.* She'd bought the matching insulated bottles especially for the honeymoon. *Damn*, he thought. *Nothing is going right.*

He waited until the flight attendants came around with water, then glanced at Thelma to make sure she was asleep before taking out his kidney and pain pills and swallowing them.

OVERLOOKING WAIKIKI BEACH, Saman leaned against the hotel balcony's iron rail. Below, tourists arranged chairs and towels on the sand in the early morning sun. Their first week in Hawaii had passed like a wave crashing.

Thelma came outside wearing a plush, white hotel robe. Her long blond hair hung wet from the shower. "I wish I could keep this," she said, standing beside him, rubbing the fabric of the bathrobe.

"Take it."

"No, they'll charge our room like a hundred dollars."

"Oh." He stared at the beach. He didn't want to think about money. His mind filled with anxiety when he calculated how much they'd charged to their credit card since arriving to Oahu.

"I was thinking we could go to that Shangri La place today," Thelma said.

"Where?"

"The Shangri La Museum? It's on every top list for Oahu. It's this mansion of Islamic Art that's part of the Honolulu Art Museum.

Saman furrowed his eyebrows, "Islamic art? Shouldn't we see some Hawaiian art?"

"It's supposed to be awesome. It used to belong to a wealthy woman who collected Arabic art. Actually, it sounds like the Bonnet House, remember, where we went on our first date?"

"Of course." The Bonnet House was a mansion and museum in Fort Lauderdale, also a former home of a wealthy, eccentric woman who collected art. Thelma had photographed him there.

"They have an artist residency program and dance performances and stuff."

"Whatever you want, babe." He kissed her again, hoping he could get through the day without another panic attack.

NOT FAR FROM WAIKIKI, the Shangri La Museum sprawled out over several acres on a dramatic seaside cliff.

"Wow," Thelma said, as they pulled up in the museum bus. "This property must be worth millions."

Cement walls surrounded the estate. Tall, skinny pine trees, star-shaped flower beds, and a terrace of hedges led to an Olympic-sized turquoise swimming pool. Arched windows and white walls gave the mansion a modern, but Moroccan aesthetic. Queen palms sprouted on the property's corners. Beyond the edge of the manicured yard, the Pacific Ocean shimmered like a mirror to the sky.

"Beautiful," Thelma breathed. "This entire building is a work of art." Two life-size stone camels flanked the front door. Traditional Arabic flute and drum music played as they entered.

"*Salam Aloha*," said a tall, thin man with brown skin, wearing a round, white and green *kufi*, the hat worn by devout Muslim men.

"*Salam Aloha*," Thelma repeated.

Saman said nothing. The word '*Salam,*' which meant peace, made his blood pressure rise. While his mother embraced Islam, having been raised in the faith, Saman's father had blamed the religion for his brother's death. The Islamic Revolutionary Guard in Iran had executed Saman's uncle in the name of that religion of "peace," shot him from overhead in a mass grave to avoid moving his dead body. Saman's father suffered from survivor's guilt and never discussed the reasons why his brother had been executed. Saman only knew his uncle from old stories about his musical talent. He'd been a concert pianist and teacher before his death.

The museum guide welcomed them to wait for the tour to begin at the first exhibition's entrance. "We will have a special presentation," the guide said. "Every few months we bring different modern artists from the Muslim world to work and live here, to create experiences for the museum. This month, we have Kurdish conceptual photographer and filmmaker, Azade Kaya."

"Ooh, a photographer," Thelma whispered.

Saman nodded. At least they would see modern art instead of old pottery.

Thelma read about the museum while they waited. "This place has a crazy story. The owner, Doris Duke, was a wealthy tobacco heiress. They called her 'The Richest Little Girl in the World.' She married an American diplomat, and they built this house after their honeymoon to the Middle East. She brought all this art here by boat in the 1940s."

Saman gazed at the ornate tiles, crystal chandeliers, and intricate Persian rugs covering every surface. "I bet that was quite a challenge."

"It also says she got addicted to painkillers after a facelift, then met a woman who claimed to be the reincarnation of her still-born baby. That woman tried to claim this estate when Doris died, but instead, she left 1.3 billion dollars to her alcoholic butler as the executor for her will."

"One lucky butler."

"Right, but there were lawsuits, so he couldn't keep it and drank himself to death."

"Dark," Saman said, looking out the window to the million-dollar ocean view. Rich people could have everything and still be miserable.

"Let's begin," the guide said. "First, we have the foyer, which represents a transition between who you are now, and who you want to be. Here you will meet Kurdish photographer, Azade Kaya. She will lead you through the rest of the tour."

Saman and Thelma followed the group past wood carvings and window cutouts painted deep red, displaying bright blue vases. Orange satin couches bordered the walls, and green-tinted glass lanterns, the size of coconuts, hung in rows from the ceiling. At the rear of the room, on a platform, a young woman waited with long, thick black hair, crimson lips, and pale skin. She wore a floor-length, maroon velvet dress and a canary-yellow silk vest.

"Welcome," the woman said, flourishing long, red nails, "I am Azade. This is a room of passage. Here you begin your change, from reality to fantasy, from ancient myth to modern art. I am a Kurdish conceptual artist, though I grew up in Tehran, Iran." Her voice was low and thick, like she was born to narrate ghost stories.

Thelma squeezed his hand and he squeezed back. She was always trying to interest him in Iranian things, as if it would bring him closer to his heritage or something. Saman didn't understand her motivation to reconnect him to a place his family had fled.

"Now," Azade said, pointing to the next room, "on this

door there is an inscription. It says, 'Shine light on your dark abode, perfume your mind.'" She lit a long stick of incense. A sweet, floral scent wafted through the air. "This door came from Tehran, where the first British Ambassador to Iran commissioned it in 1813. Thus, it is a true merging of Middle Eastern and Western tradition, and the perfect beginning to our journey."

Saman whispered to Thelma, "Guess they thought they were all going to be friends with Iran back then."

Thelma scowled and put her finger to her lips to shhh him.

They reached a marble fountain covered in precious gemstones, then a room with sapphire walls and a blue sofa. Azade pointed out various artifacts, including a ceramic prayer niche from an ancient tomb in Iran.

Next, the photographer led them to an expansive bedroom with two extra-long beds with red velvet duvets. An enormous Arabian-styled crystal chandelier cast spots of light on the Persian rugs covering the tile floor. Black curtains blocked out the sunlight and created a dramatic effect. Portraits hung from the walls. Saman noticed the pictures moved slightly. They were not photographs, he realized, but large screens showing almost-still videos. Each video portrait displayed a fantastic and hyper-realistic scene from Persian mythology. In the first image, a blond man in the forest, wearing a suit and armor made from leopard fur, held a silver sword with a thick, leg-long blade.

Azade addressed the group, "In this series, called, *Eyes or Stones?* I've mixed American models into our ancient mythological images not only to confuse the meaning, but to confuse the religious extremists. Is this *haram*? Is this forbidden in Islam? Is this blasphemy? Or is this a western actor in an unknown role? What new meaning do these images create?"

Kurdish traditional music played in the background. Saman could see that Thelma was mesmerized by the floor-to-ceiling video portraits.

"Enjoy this room as long as you like," Azade said. "I will be in the garden if you have any questions. Use the head-phones beside the video portraits to hear the Persian myths in English."

"This is so cool," Thelma whispered to Saman.

Saman agreed. He'd never seen anything like the videos. The blond man with the sword was a portrait of *Rostam*, a famous warrior known for wearing a leopard skin suit. The next image was a white horse wading through a pool of mercury water. In another, a young man on a throne clutched a peacock. Thelma was listening to the recording for a man painted blue, holding a club, and wearing red horns on his head. A *jiin*, an Islamic demon, Saman thought. He stopped in front of a dark-haired child dressed like a sun with a yellow crown of spikes. The child, who resembled his niece, Suri, squeezed a stuffed animal of a lion to her chest and scowled at the camera.

Thelma touched his shoulder, "Look at this one. It reminds me of the picture I took of you with the feathers."

Saman followed her to the image of an older man with a long, white beard and a square hat posed in a desert land-scape. Naked above the waist, the model wore a thick costume of bird's feathers in purple and yellow that spread from his hips like an eagle in flight. Saman recognized the man as the *Faravahar*, a Zoroastrian icon from ancient Persia. *Why didn't I realize this connection before?* He wondered. Despite having seen the Faravahar countless times, the link hadn't dawned on him.

Thelma handed him the portrait's headphones, "Listen."

The voice of Azade, the artist, spoke, and heavy string instruments played cinematic music.

> *"We all have two sides, two ends, our*
> *crown and our root, the flowers and*
> *the seed.*
> *The Faravahar is an animal and a man,*
> *instinct and ego.*
> *One is good and one is bad.*
> *Ahura Mazda is the God of The Good,*
> *and Ahreeman is the God of The Bad.*
> *The Faravahar is the balance between*
> *them. Balance is salvation.*
> *But this dichotomy is a lie, because*
> *nothing is absolute.*
> *The Faravahar wields a ring of power —*
> *intellect.*
> *Universal intelligence is where true*
> *power lies."*

Saman took off the headphones. He rubbed his eyes. Suddenly, he was exhausted, and the gallery felt claustrophobic.

Thelma frowned, "You should listen to the whole thing. It's really good."

"That story is common knowledge for Persians."

"Maybe you were subconsciously thinking about it when you had the vision of yourself in the feathers? I could have seen this before too. Do you think that's why your photo resonated with people?"

Saman didn't feel like thinking. "I don't know. It's a coincidence."

Thelma cocked her head to the side and looked at him with a disappointed expression "Seems like a pretty big coincidence."

He shrugged, "I'm going outside." As he left the gallery, his eye caught a video near the exit. An aging African woman in a black cloak carried a basket in a dim jungle. She wore artificial vampire teeth and fake blood rimmed her lips. In the basket, raw meat, slick with body fluids, reflected in the camera's flash.

Saman shuddered. *Now, that's a coincidence. Had Thelma seen that portrait? Did she remember the story of Al?* He'd thought about it many times since the mushroom ceremony with Maria. *Why is this shit following me?* Goosebumps rose on his forearm. *What were the odds that he'd see Al on his honeymoon?* With each step, he felt less certain about reality.

At the edge of the garden's perimeter, he leaned over a stone wall and studied the waves crashing below. Part of him considered what it would be like to jump over the wall. He'd never do it, but sometimes it felt like life only delayed death. He spread his fingers on the gray stone for a moment, then glanced around to check if Thelma was outside. She wasn't. He swallowed an Oxy from his pocket. He'd planned to finish the pills before leaving Oahu for the Big Island, but that would be tomorrow. There were still ten left. It didn't make sense to throw them out. He swallowed a second one. Then went to look for a shade tree to escape the blistering sun while he waited for Thelma.

As he walked across the garden, Azade approached him. "Hi. You're Persian, aren't you?" she said, smiling.

He stopped and squinted at her through his sunglasses, "You guessed it."

"I can always tell, as I'm sure you can too. And you don't see many Iranians here in Hawaii."

"Is that so?"

"Well, I haven't." She paused. "You didn't stay long inside. Did you find the art offensive?"

Saman let out a snort, "Offensive? Me? No. I'm not that kind of Iranian. I'm sure some would. You're brave to make those."

"Luckily, few people here understand them." She grinned, "Anyway, I came here for the free trip to Hawaii. I'm not Muslim," she laughed.

He cracked a smile, then said, "I'm Saman. I'm an audio engineer."

"Oh, that's so cool. I should get your contact. I always need music help for my art. You live here?"

"No, in Florida. What about you?"

"New York, but I don't think I'm going back. I like it here."

"Nice," Saman said, "Well, I can give you my number, for your next project."

Azade smiled and tilted her head down, then looked at him through her long, black eyelashes, "That would be great."

Heat warmed his cheeks. *Was she flirting with him?* It had been a while since he'd interacted with an unknown Iranian female. The experience felt strange and somehow wrong.

Still, he gave her his number.

"Thanks," she said. "Okay, I better go talk to the other visitors. It was nice to meet you." She reached out her hand and he shook it. Her palm was soft and warm. He worried that his was sweaty.

"Nice to meet you," he mumbled.

"I'm sure I'll see you again." She connected with his eyes, tilted her chin to the side and smiled, slightly parting her red lips, then she dropped his palm and walked away.

Saman's heart pounded. *What had that been about? She must be lonely,* he thought. *Why did I give her my number? I should have told her I was married.* But it was too late, she was already talking to someone else.

Thirty minutes passed before Thelma found him under a tree.

"Finally," he said.

"Seriously, Saman? You barely looked at the pictures."

"I looked at all of them."

"It's disrespectful to the photographer, and I wanted to experience this with you, but you left me by myself."

"You seemed fine. What's your problem?" He hadn't realized she was upset that he'd left.

"My problem?" She shook her head, "What's your problem?"

Saman sighed. "Come on, don't give me a hard time. I'm not interested in this kind of stuff. You know that. It legitimizes a violent religion."

"There are peaceful Muslims."

"No amount of modernization can fix fundamentally bad ideas."

"Well, you don't have to be rude. You could have stayed inside with me and looked around."

Saman stood, "Let's go."

"It's a cultural landmark." Thelma shook her head. "What's going on with you? If you can't be happy on our honeymoon, when will you be happy?"

"Do we have to do this now?" Saman snapped.

"It's like you hate your own culture. You don't give things a chance."

"That's not true."

She followed him to the parking lot. "I think you need to go back to therapy. You're angry all the time."

Saman ignored her. "When does the next bus leave?"

"Please don't change the subject."

Saman rubbed off sweat that beaded across his forehead in the thick humid air. *What was Thelma's issue anyway? Why can't she just let me be?*

"You're never happy. Nothing interests you. It isn't good. You should go back to Dr. Diaz," she continued.

"That guy was an idiot."

"Then see someone else, but you need to do something. You're clearly depressed."

"No shit," Saman mumbled. He wanted the conversation to end.

"You have collective trauma from your dad and mom, probably from all your Iranian relatives."

Saman tried to conceal his annoyance. *How dare she armchair diagnose him? He had every reason to feel the way he did. He wasn't going back to therapy, no way. It was a waste of money.*

Thelma rambled about ancestral trauma and the generational effects of war while he pretended to listen. With each word, the Oxy pills permeated his bloodstream, then his brain. Like a handful of sand thrown into the sea they dissolved her complaints away.

9

From their table for two, Thelma admired the sun, hung like an orange balloon over the Pacific, filling the atmosphere with blush and amber hues. For their last night in Oahu, she'd booked dinner at an in-demand beachfront restaurant with a large outdoor deck. Triangle silhouettes of passing sailboats accentuated the postcard view and the evening breeze refreshed Thelma's semi-sunburnt shoulders, bare in her strapless floral dress.

Saman sat across from her but studied the menu instead of the sunset. Since their fight at the Shangri La Museum, he seemed far away, as if he'd checked out of his brain like a hotel room.

The waiter approached with a tall blue bottle of sparkling water and filled their glasses. "Are you ready to order? Or do you need another moment?" He wore a bright red and black, flowered Hawaiian shirt.

"Yes," Thelma said. "We will do the prix fixe."

"Excellent," the waiter replied.

They both selected their choices from the menu, lamb for Saman and fish for herself.

"And is it a special occasion?" the waiter asked.

Thelma looked at Saman.

"Yes, our anniversary," Saman said.

Thelma blinked. It wasn't their anniversary. She nudged him under the table with her foot.

"I mean honeymoon," Saman laughed. "Sorry, I'm getting ahead of myself."

The waiter laughed, "Both romantic occasions. I'll add something extra for you." He winked then whisked away their menus.

As the dusk settled, yellow fairy lights sparkled from the tree branches around the terrace.

Thelma reached for Saman's hand across the table and he turned his palm over to welcome her touch.

"I'm sorry about earlier," Saman suddenly offered. "I don't know why, but the art agitated me."

"It's okay," Thelma said.

"I love," he said.

"I love you, too."

They sat in silence, experiencing each other's skin on their hands.

"Did you see the one of Al?" Saman finally asked.

"Al?" Thelma sipped her water.

Before he could answer the waiter returned carrying two flutes of sparkling champagne with a splash of red at the bottom and a twist of lemon at the top.

"For the lovely honeymoon couple," he said, setting down the glasses. "A complimentary Kir Royal for you both."

"Oh wow, that's fancy," Thelma gushed. Though Saman was not supposed to drink too much alcohol, and she rarely drank, the presentation of the champagne was sweet and unexpected.

"Let's toast," Thelma said, raising her glass.

Saman raised his champagne, "To you."

"To you."

And with the clink of their glasses, they let the tension from the afternoon slip away like the day.

The conversation turned to everything they wanted to do together, from planting a butterfly garden to climbing Machu Picchu.

Feeling free and happy, Thelma ordered another Kir Royale and then another. Saman drank a second glass of champagne as well.

With glossy eyes he said, "You're feeling fun tonight," as the waiter brought a third champagne.

She laughed and toasted the beach. "To Hawaii!"

With desert she drank a fourth champagne. *Why not?* she thought.

"We should have bought a bottle," Saman said, yawning.

The waiter returned carrying a chocolate volcano with a lit candle in it. "Happy Honeymoon!" He exclaimed, as he set the glowing mound of cake in between them.

"Ooh," Thelma squealed.

"I don't know if I can take another bite," Saman said, yawning again, "I'm stuffed."

"Always room for chocolate," Thelma blew out the candle and dipped her fork into the warm fudge. It tasted like cherries and hot cocoa on her tongue.

"Let's go for a walk on the beach," she said, in between bites.

"I don't know, I'm fading."

"Come on, a short one."

By the time they paid the bill, Saman looked half asleep, but Thelma felt like she could dance all night.

"You don't even want to know how much that cost,"

Saman shook his head as they left the restaurant's seating area.

"No, I don't!" she said. Fueled by sugar and champagne, she linked her arm through his and drug him to the sandy beach. Thelma almost tripped, trying to get off her platform heels.

"Woah there," Saman laughed, "Are you drunk?"

"Maybe," she giggled. She poked his stomach and laughed. "Come and get me." She ran towards the ocean. Stopping at the edge of the waves, Thelma gazed at the moonlit sea. Stars shimmered overhead. Saman wrapped his arms around her from behind and kissed her neck. Heat flooded her body and pooled in her pelvis. Aroused by his kisses, she reached around and rubbed the front seam of his pants with her palm.

"Hey there," Saman said.

He was soft. She found his penis inside the fabric and stroked it with her fingertips, trying to wake up his erection.

He cupped one of her breasts in his hand and sucked on her earlobe. Then he turned her around and kissed her on the lips. A wave licked their feet with cool water. Her sex throbbed with desire for him. Saman slid his tongue into her mouth and she pressed his warm body against her. Still, he wasn't hard. She rubbed him again. *Come on,* she thought.

"Hey, slow down, drunky," he said.

She giggled. "I'm so wet," she whispered.

"Perv," Saman looked around, "someone might see us."

"There isn't anyone here and it's dark. She kissed his mouth, tasting the chocolate cake and champagne on his tongue as hers slid between his lips. She wanted him inside her. If only the hotel was closer. "Touch me," she said, breathing hot breath onto his skin.

He reached his hand up her dress and traced his fingertips over the thin fabric covering her vagina. She murmured, "Hmm." It felt so good. She kissed him again, harder and he slid her lace panties to the side. Her lips parted for him and she ached with pleasure as he entered her body with his finger. "Oh, yes!" Her own wetness dampened the edges of her thighs as he swirled his finger inside her, opening her more and more, making her heart pound and her breath race.

He added a second finger. She grabbed onto his shoulder and looked around again. *Would anyone see them?* But it was dark, and they were far from the restaurant's amber glow.

He thrust his hand deep inside her, gripping her and tugging her towards him. She hung on tight to his back and moved her pelvis in rhythm with the push and pull of his hand. The champagne swam in her blood like fish, moving heat into her erect nipples. He squeezed her pubic mound against the palm of his hand, wiggling his fingers in her, and pressing her hard nipple between his fingers with his other hand.

"Oh, my God, I'm going to cum," she whispered in his ear.

"Cum," he said, moving his lips to her earlobe, sucking again on her soft skin, filling her entire body with hot sensation. She leaned into him. Her crotch pulsed like a heartbeat. The sound of pleasure escaped her lips. He stifled the moaning noises she made with his hand over her mouth. Her legs shook with sexual energy, releasing her orgasm in a burst of muscle contractions. Like warm honey on bread, she came in his hands.

10

The Big Island's black and amber beaches curved around jagged craters and green peaks like finger-prints pressed into the sea. The aircraft's loud engine drowned out any potential conversations. Thelma's head pounded from the lingering effects of last night's champagne. *Why did I drink so much?* She chastised herself, especially so soon before a ceremony, it wasn't good to consume alcohol. Nauseous, she leaned her pounding forehead against the airplane's oval window, straining to see past the wing, to take in the full beauty of the island below. A field of black lava bordered the runway. The level of nowhere was staggering. *This is the end of the earth,* she thought, feeling a mix of wonderment and apprehension.

Saman was on the other side of the plane's narrow aisle. She hoped he was okay. Between the jet lag, the overpriced food, and the throngs of Japanese tourists on Oahu, their magical Hawaii honeymoon was not as fantastic as she'd envisioned. Still, excitement stirred in her stomach. Soon they would touch down on the southernmost landmass of the United States. More than her hangover, or the slight anxiety she always felt when flying over the ocean, this was the feeling she got before plant medicine ceremonies — a nervous energy, the hope for an eventful encounter with *The Divine*. She could not wait to get to Bāne Kama's house for their mushroom ceremony.

As they began their descent to the Kona airport, gliding over miles of hardened, jet-black lava, rainbow reflections glimmered in the foam between the ocean's waves. Thelma took out her camera and snapped a photo of the dancing, prismatic, multi-colored light hovering under the plane before they lurched to a stop on the tarmac. Only a thin strip of ground separated them from the sparkling South Pacific.

Once stopped, passengers unstrapped their seat belts and got their bags out of the overhead bins.

Saman leaned towards Thelma and raised his eyebrows, "Here we are."

She nodded, though she felt like throwing up. At least he seemed less hungover than she was. As they de-boarded, walking carefully down portable aluminum steps directly onto the tarmac, her breath caught in her chest; the Kona airport was like no other airport she had ever seen. Thatched roofs covered open-air shops and baggage claim areas.

"This is wild," Saman said. "It's more like Disney World than an airport."

"It really does look like the entrance to Animal Kingdom," Thelma observed, "What happens when it rains?"

The afternoon sun was scorching and bright, and Thelma wished she'd put on sunblock. She never imagined the possibility of getting sunburnt inside an airport. She envied Saman's ability to tan without burning.

After grabbing their checked bags, they boarded a

shuttle bus to the rental car company, along with everyone else from their flight. While it would have been closer to Bāne Kama's place to fly into Hilo, the flights to Kona had been much cheaper, even with the car rental.

"Guess no locals on the plane, huh?" Saman said to Thelma in line.

"I wonder what sort of person is local here?"

"I wonder how humans even found this place?"

After twenty minutes in line, an Asian man greeted them with a grin at the rental car counter, "Aloha. Do you have a reservation?"

Thelma gave him her confirmation number.

"Oh, only five days? Too bad," the man said, "not enough time to enjoy the island."

Thelma shrugged, "We'll make the most of it."

"You selected a sedan, but I recommend you upgrade to an SUV. We've had a lot of rain lately and you may need four-wheel drive."

"Thank you, but that won't be necessary." Saman said.

"Where do you plan to go?" the car rental agent asked.

"Towards Hilo," Thelma answered.

The man laughed, "Definitely take the four-wheel drive. There are eight climate zones on this Island. It could be sunny here and raining there. I'll tell you what, I'll give you guys a great deal. I know honeymooners when I see them." He winked, "And to be honest, the car you booked hasn't been returned, so it's your lucky day. I've got a Jeep Wrangler for you. All you have to do is pay the change fee."

Thelma looked at Saman for confirmation.

"How much is the change fee?"

"Fifty dollars."

"We can swing that," Thelma said, before Saman could say no. "Thank you so much."

Saman raised his eyebrows but stepped back and let her take over the rest of the transaction.

A brand-new, forest-green Jeep Wrangler convertible with gigantic tires and tan leather seats waited for them outside.

"Seriously!" Saman exclaimed, "I've wanted to drive one of these since I was a little kid." He squeezed Thelma's shoulders and gave her a kiss. "I'm glad this worked out."

"This is very cool. I've never ridden in one before."

Saman threw their luggage in the back of the Jeep. "Let's take the top down."

As he undid the cover, Thelma admired his long black hair and bronze arms. He was sexy and masculine beside the jacked-up Wrangler.

With the excitement of a little boy on a go-cart, Saman steered onto the road. Thelma turned on the Jeep's radio and flipped through the channels, settling on a reggae station, which seemed appropriate for the landscape. As they left the suburban area of Kona and headed into the countryside, Thelma said, "Finally, this feels like we're in the real Hawaii." Her blond hair whipped around her face. Hardened lava coated the Big Island's sloping hills like black buttercream. She pulled out her camera and clicked a shot of Saman driving the Jeep. "Have you ever seen any place like this before?"

Saman shook his head, "No, and I'm glad I didn't look at pictures before we came, so I can see it for the first time."

She snapped another picture. It was true, the Internet could ruin surprises. It allowed you see everything without going yourself. Maybe that was another reason she liked the plant medicine ceremonies. You couldn't predict what would appear, nor could you post it on Instagram. There was no Google search for your own visions.

As they climbed higher into the mountains, she asked, "Do you know where you're going?"

"Sort of. Can you run the GPS?"

"I'm not getting any cell service."

"The rental car guy gave us a map."

Rainforest now surrounded the road. In the distance, gray clouds with dark centers formed, resting above the treetops.

Thelma unfolded the paper map and scrutinized it. They passed a large school.

"Did that say Keanu High School?" she asked, "like Keanu Reeves?"

"You wish!" Saman chuckled.

Thelma rolled her eyes.

The road split in the distance. "There!" she pointed, "turn left there."

Saman did, and they passed cattle farms and fenced ranches. Roadside signs advertised donuts and locally-raised steak. After driving for an hour, the landscape changed to dense jungle. Bridges and valleys, thick and emerald, flew by the Jeep's windows.

"Look, a waterfall," Thelma exclaimed, pointing to a cascade on a hill. They sloped down a paved street, and the ocean reappeared.

"Wow," Saman said. "We're already on the other side of the island."

As if on cue, the weather flipped; rain pelted with such sudden intensity that before Saman could put up the Jeep's top, they were soaking wet.

"Our bags are getting drenched!" Thelma shouted.

"I can't stop here," Saman yelled. "The road's too narrow."

Wind blew rain inside the jeep, spraying them with

water. Saman drove a few minutes further, then veered to the side. Thelma couldn't tell if they were parking on grass or a curb. A truck whizzed past them, going the other way. Saman leapt out of the Jeep, and Thelma pulled off her sweater and held it over her head to protect herself from the hammering storm. Thunder boomed in the sky.

"Is there a button up there?" Saman yanked at the canvas top's folding metal poles, struggling to raise the top. "It's stuck."

Rain puddled in the seat and Thelma pulled on the other side of the top. Lighting flashed. Saman tried again to force the top up.

"Saman!" She jumped out of the car to help him and gasped; the road dropped off dramatically. They were centimeters away from rolling over the edge of a steep ravine.

"We've got to get out of here!" She yelled and climbed back inside the vehicle. "Saman!"

He didn't answer. Unable to see him, Thelma stood to get a better view. *Oh, my God,* she thought. *What if he fell into the ditch?* "Saman!" she shouted again. As if in response, the Jeep's canvas top flew toward her. Before she could move, the metal bar smacked her in the face. Thelma fell backwards and hit her head on the dashboard. "Owe!" she shrieked, clutching at her face. Her left eye burned, and she tasted the metallic flavor of blood streaming from her throbbing nose.

Saman jumped into the driver's seat, his shoes sloshing water around the gas pedal and brakes. "Oh, shit! Did that hit you? Are you okay?" He reached for her hand.

"I'm fine," she cried, "Just move. This isn't safe. We're right on the edge of a ravine."

Saman jerked the jeep onto the road and drove through the rushing rain.

"I'm so sorry, babe, I didn't mean to hit you. Are you bleeding?"

"Just my nose."

"I'll stop at the next gas station."

She shook her head. "It's okay, I have tissues in my purse." Pain droned in her skull and her eyelid swelled. She touched the space between her lip and nose; blood coated her fingers. *So much for using this trip to take a new photo series of the ocean,* she thought. I'll be lucky if I'm not blind in one eye. Wet and cold, she wanted to cry. Constant rain had plagued their entire first year of marriage. *Was it from climate change, or bad luck?*

They drove in silence. Dramatic bolts of lightning lit the gray sky. *This would be beautiful if my eye wasn't bleeding,* Thelma thought. *And were they lost?* Saman's expression wasn't encouraging her. He gripped the steering wheel and furtively checked the paper map.

"I missed a turn," he said, slowing his speed.

Thelma grimaced. Her nose, eye, and cheek ached.

After a few minutes, Saman found a driveway and made a U-turn. They drove another hour. The magic of their arrival faded.

Thelma yawned. "Babe, are we almost there?" She tried to sound neutral and calm. The last thing she wanted was to stress out Saman.

Before answering, he made a sharp turn and took the Jeep down a bumpy, gravel lane. Thelma clutched the Jeep's roll bar as they jolted over the rough terrain.

"Saman? Do you know where we are?"

He sighed, "Ye of little faith. We're here."

They were on a dirt road the width of the jeep. In the

dark rain, their headlights illuminated a cube-shaped cement structure with a neon sign that said, *"Cubic Cabana"* in pink, tubular letters. She recognized it from the rental property's photos. Thelma exhaled.

"You have to trust me, wifey. My sense of direction is impeccable. Now, let's take a look at your face. I'm so sorry that happened."

"That's okay. Let's do it inside, please. I'm exhausted, and my nose hurts. I need some Advil." She held her hand steady over her eye socket. It felt like if she moved it her retina might fall out.

"I have some prescription painkillers."

Thelma furrowed her brow then winced from the pain the movement caused. "Really? You're still taking those?"

"No. I brought them to help me sleep on the plane; they make me drowsy."

"I wish I'd known; I would have taken one sooner. Yes, can I have one?"

Saman got his book bag from the backseat and fished out the pill container.

She swallowed the pill dry. "How strong are these? Do I need two?"

"Pretty strong; one should be fine. Do you think your nose is broken?"

"I hope not." *Fuck.* She hadn't even considered that her nose might be broken. A welt was forming on the back of her head from where she'd slammed into the dashboard.

They dragged their damp luggage to the front door. She could hear the ocean, but with the thick clouds covering the moon, it was hard to see the landscape.

Saman punched in the house's entry code and they stepped inside an open-concept kitchen with orange tile floors. Saman switched on more lights. Modern furniture filled the living room and a six-foot statue of a Rubik's cube painted with Hawaiian flowers rested on a pedestal by a floor-to-ceiling window.

"This place is pretty cool," Saman said.

"I love the art," Thelma dropped her hand to her side, exposing her eye.

"Oh honey, that doesn't look good."

She inched away from him, "What? Oh God, please tell me my eyeball isn't like hanging out."

He scrunched his face. "I think you should go to the bathroom and check it out."

Thelma found a bathroom and catching sight of herself in the mirror, she gasped. A dark purple bruise welled around her bloodshot eye. The whites of her eyeball leaked red blood. Yellowish puss oozed and pooled on her lower eyelash. The Jeep's top had scraped the bridge of her nose and had cut her cheek. Her heart pounded. *What if this has done permanent damage? Would this affect her photography?* The wounded eye was like a slimy, skinned fish. She shuddered.

Saman came in behind her with ice wrapped in a dish towel.

She pressed it to her face. "A freaking black eye, just what I needed for our honeymoon pictures."

"Photoshop?" he offered with a pained expression.

"And hopefully there won't be any boats going by while we pee because there is no privacy here at all." She gestured to the window by the toilet. The bathroom was all glass.

Saman shrugged, "Give the sailors a little treat."

"Hope they like pirates." She pointed to her eye.

He laughed, then took her hand, "Should I kiss it and make it better?"

"Ew, barf, please don't."

He embraced her and rubbed her back. She leaned into his chest as he moved his fingers lower and squeezed her bottom, "What if I kiss you somewhere else?"

She rested against him. "Mmm, that sounds appealing, but I'm pretty dirty. I need a shower."

"I can wait."

Under the welcome heat of the shower, she scrubbed the airplane grime off her body, then toweled herself dry. Tan lines from her bathing suit turned her firm breasts into matching white pyramids on her lean, naked body.

As she stepped out of the bathroom, Saman slid off his pants and boxer shorts. His tall frame looked like that of a long-distance runner's. The scar from his kidney surgery glimmered on his ridged abdomen. She'd never realized how big a kidney was before she'd seen the long hole it left in him. Reclining on the bed naked, Saman climbed onto her like a jaguar, and she wrapped her arms around his smooth torso. "I love you," she whispered and let her towel fall onto the bed, revealing her wet, erect nipples. The tiny hairs on her flat stomach raised as Saman kissed her breasts.

"I love you, too." Saman pressed his erection into the thin strip of blond pubic hair leading to her vagina. All her muscles relaxed, and pleasure traveled from his kiss to every part of her body. The stress of the car ride faded and all her pain subsided.

He filled his mouth with her nipple.

"Mmm," she murmured. It was too much. She touched the top of his head, and gently pushed him down, urging him to move lower.

He slid his lips to her navel. Drawing a line with his tongue from her belly button to the top of her pubic bone.

The painkillers made the room feel like a dream. She giggled, "That tickles."

Saman worked his mouth around the edge of her labia, kissing her, and outlining circles with his tongue.

She wanted all the love he could give her. As he slid his tongue in and out of her, she caressed his neck with the tips of her nails. He squeezed her hips hard in his palms and thrust his mouth deeper into her warm body. Moaning with ecstasy, she gripped onto him and tightened her thighs around his ribs.

"That feels so fucking good," she whispered. Saman pushed his tongue in harder and sucked on her clitoris. She dug her nails into his back. As she neared climax, he slid on her tingling skin, rubbing his hardened penis on her stomach, then he sank himself into the space between her thighs. As his cock entered her, she cried out with pleasure and immediately fell into the beginning of an orgasm. He pushed in further and held himself against her. She melted. Unable to control herself, Thelma climaxed, hard; her body convulsed. The walls of her vagina pulsed around Saman and she shrieked with sexual release.

"There you go," he whispered. "That was fast."

Her entire body shook and spasmed. He thrust himself into her again, then again, and again. He squeezed her flesh in his hands and pumped into her hard. She shrieked and moaned, overwhelmed by the sensations, his force, and the rapid thrusts. Then just as she couldn't take anymore, his semen rushed inside her, a warm flow of liquid as his body collapsed onto her breasts. Bliss washed over her. He shuddered and she held him.

"I needed that," she breathed, panting.

"I love you."

"I love you, too." Her pain had all disappeared. She

smiled with her eyes closed. He pulled out and flopped beside her on the bed, then turned to spoon her body, draping his leg in between her wet thighs. She closed her eyes and grabbed his hand with hers. She was his, entirely his, in that moment, and for the rest of time.

11

Sunlight glared at Thelma's aching eye through the glass wall of the cube house's bedroom. Saman slept beside her, his tan figure tangled in the white sheets.

Feeling exposed, she rose and wrapped herself in a towel. In the bathroom mirror, her eye bulged red and swollen. A purple bruise stretched across her nose and cheek. *This isn't good,* she thought, *damn, this sucks.* The last thing she wanted to do was waste a day of their honeymoon at a doctor's office. She put on sunglasses, hoping they would help with her hurt eye's sensitivity, and unlocked a sliding glass door in the living room. Outside, hardened lava surrounded the cube, the color of crude oil, with sprigs of weeds and tiny pink flowers popping up every couple of feet in the molten crust's cracks. Beyond the black rock, the Pacific Ocean radiated white mist like a mirage.

They were much closer to the coast than she'd realized last night. The brightly colored, yet stark, landscape left her still and awe-struck. The air smelled of honeysuckle and sea salt. The cliff she stood on jutted out into a peacock-blue sky. Choppy, with high waves, the ocean appeared too dangerous for swimming. Under her bare feet, the lava felt hot and sharp. She went back inside and put on flip-flops. Then, careful not to fall, she made her way towards the ocean.

Two gray Adirondack chairs and a wrought-iron side table rested on the rocks facing the water. As Thelma was about to sit, she heard a man's voice.

"Good morning!"

Thelma whipped around, clutching the towel tighter to her body, suddenly wishing she'd gotten dressed.

"Sorry, I didn't mean to startle you," the man said.

She blinked. A young guy, maybe in his late twenties or early thirties, with shaggy blond hair, a gold tan, and mirror-tinted sporty sunglasses grinned and waived. He wore board shorts and a tank top, but no shoes.

"You must be Thelma," he said.

"Yes. Sorry, you caught me off guard. Are you the owner of the guest house?" She hugged her towel to her chest. In awe of the ocean, she'd not fully registered that their cube house was down the hill from a larger house.

"No, the owner is my girlfriend, but she's a busy doctor, so I help her out with things, manage the place. You just missed her. She wanted to come say hello, but she had to scoot off to work."

A doctor? It was too good to be true. Maybe the owner could examine her eye?

"I'm Dan," the man said, in what she identified as an Australian accent. He came closer.

How is he walking on this lava? She wondered as she shook his hand. "Nice to meet you."

"Anyway, my girlfriend, Roberta, she's from Florida too, from West Palm Beach. That's where you're from right?"

Thelma nodded. "Well, I'm from New England, but I live in Florida now and we are pretty close to West Palm."

"We don't get many Floridians here, so we wanted to invite you guys for some happy hour drinks tonight by the pool." He motioned behind him to a narrow, rectangular pool in front of the main house, built into the black lava rock.

"That's very kind of you," she hesitated, "and actually, I could really use a doctor — I hurt my eye yesterday."

"Oh, no." He leaned his head sideways, trying to see under her sunglasses.

"It's not a pleasant sight," she said, embarrassed.

He nodded. "I'm sure Roberta could take a look. What happened?"

"Thelma?" Saman's voice interrupted her before she could respond. She turned to see Saman walking from the cube house with a quizzical expression.

"Oh, hello, mate," Dan pivoted and went to shake hands with Saman. "I wanted to invite you and the misses over for a drink this evening by the pool."

"His girlfriend is a doctor," Thelma added.

"Hi," Saman said. Thelma couldn't tell if he was half-asleep or half-annoyed. She moved to his side and looped her arm around his elbow.

"He said maybe she can examine my eye." She looked at Saman.

"Okay, yes," Saman said, "sure."

"Great," Dan grinned. "Alright then, see you both this evening at sunset." He tipped his head and bounded away over the lava rocks like a kangaroo.

Saman and Thelma exchanged comical glances.

"That guy seemed like a weirdo," Saman said, scowling.

"I guess he was trying to be friendly."

"Nah, he was checking you out," Saman yawned. "But it's okay, I would too." He poked her playfully in the side then tugged at her towel. "Put some clothes on next time maybe."

She giggled and swatted his hand away. "Don't make me laugh, my face hurts."

He hugged her, "I'm so sorry about that, babe. That really sucks."

"It's okay. I'm more concerned with what we are going to eat. We should have gotten some groceries before we left town."

"Yeah, and I don't really want to drive back to Hilo."

"I thought maybe we'd go to those waterfalls? There are two different ones. We could get breakfast on the way."

Saman raised his eyebrows. "Waterfalls again? We did that on Oahu."

She frowned. "I'm here for all the waterfalls."

"I was hoping to have a chill day. I mean, look at this view." He gestured to the ocean.

"Well, we have to eat at some point."

"Check the fridge. I think I saw a plate of fruit or something wrapped in plastic."

They went back inside the house and Thelma examined the contents of the refrigerator. Excited, she pulled out a platter wrapped in plastic wrap, "They left us breakfast," she exclaimed. "That's so sweet!"

"See, no reason to leave," Saman said.

"Okay, if there's coffee, then we can stay." Thelma smiled. *Maybe they could squeeze in seeing the waterfalls on their last day.*

Saman grabbed his backpack and pulled out a packet of coffee. "Boom. I grabbed that from the hotel. That settles it! Hawaii honeymoon chill day."

Thelma shook her head, "Okay, you win. But let's at least explore a little later and see if there's a grocery store."

"Later, being the operative word," Saman said.

As Thelma unwrapped the fruit plate, the doorbell rang. Thelma and Saman looked at each other. "You answer it," she mouthed.

Saman obliged. It was Dan again, standing in the doorway with the same goofy grin.

"Hey?" Saman asked, turning back to Thelma with an oh-my-God expression.

"Hey mate, hope I'm not interrupting, but I saw your Jeep, so I thought you guys might go to Green Beach, but I wanted to tell you they've got the main road closed, so you've got to go in from the south, so plan for a longer drive." He looked around Saman to Thelma and waved at her.

"Oh, okay," Saman said, "But no, we weren't planning on it today, but thanks for the fruit and stuff in the fridge."

"Yeah, they've had it closed for weeks," Dan trailed off. Saman and Thelma stared at him in awkward silence.

"Okay then, well, I'll see you tonight, and if you want lunch there's a place close by called *Rosita's Casita*. They've got great fish tacos."

"Thanks," Saman said, still holding the door with one hand.

"Alright then, see you tonight!" Dan waved and again almost sprinted back to his own house.

Saman shut the door. "That guy is desperate for friends."

"I bet it gets lonely out here," Thelma said pouring the now hot coffee into a mug. "He's probably bored, not working, lying around the pool all day while his girlfriend works."

Saman's face fell.

Shit, I said the wrong thing, Thelma realized. She backpedaled. "I mean, I shouldn't say that. Maybe he has a job, and he's off today," then she stopped; that wasn't the right thing to say either.

"Yeah, what a loser," Saman replied sarcastically.

"I didn't mean that."

"Actually, that is what you meant."

"No, babe, come on. Please don't take this personally." She stopped. It was pointless, she'd already set him off.

"You know what, I'll go look for that grocery store after all," Saman said. Irritation oozed from each word he spoke, "I'm craving some bacon." He grabbed the Jeep's keys and headed to the front door.

"Come on, babe. Please don't be upset. I didn't mean anything personal."

He shook his head. "Whatever. It's true. I'm becoming a total loser." He left before she could respond. Thelma watched him back out of the driveway, tires churning on the gravel. She sighed. *This was not how their morning was supposed to go.* When Saman was waiting for the transplant, his turbulent moods had seemed like natural reactions to his difficult health situation, but now, post-surgery, she wondered if they were part of his innate personality. *Had his frustration and rage become a habit he was stuck in, a pattern of negativity?*

While he was never violent or unkind to her, he would berate and criticize himself with such cruelty that his self-hatred was hard for her to watch. Other times, he would withdraw, slamming doors, or disappearing from the house for extended periods. Sometimes he threw his own possessions across the room or screamed into his closet full of clothes. Minor issues generated enormous emotional reactions. Over time, she'd learned to spot the warning signs of his internal combustions. Experience had taught her to let him be when he was worked up, to say as little as possible, to wait until he chilled out on his own. Still, it was never easy to watch his meltdowns.

Stirring a sugar cube into her coffee, she took a croissant and went back outside. She navigated the jagged lava as gingerly as she avoided triggering Saman's bad moods. By the shoreline, she slumped into the chair, listening to the roar of the water as it slammed against the land. *How did we get to this point?* she wondered. *When did we start bickering all the time?* She was so tired of Saman's mood swings. *I shouldn't be alone on our honeymoon, feeling sad.* A tear dripped painfully from her hurt eye. *If he couldn't be happy now, when would he be happy? Would the mushroom ceremony help him?* Mushrooms were known to combat depression and anxiety, something Saman definitely needed. *Or would the ceremony cause him more harm?* She sometimes worried that their last ceremony and her vision of the spider had ushered in a bad omen for his surgery.

Picking up a palm-sized rock from the ground by her feet, she hurled it at the sea. It fell and disappeared in an instant, sucked under by the cerulean waves. At least she could make the best of this incredible view while she waited for him to come back and apologize, as he always did after one of his outbursts.

As she sat in silence, watching the waves, the wind and sun soothed away the hurt of Saman's abrupt departure. After a few minutes, she closed her eyes and tapped into her inner field of consciousness. While at first, she couldn't conjure visions herself, she could only receive them during plant medicine ceremonies or from dreams, now she was starting to channel visions during her waking life — using meditation.

With deep breaths, in and out, she imagined the circle of the mushroom ceremony they would attend on Saturday. She visualized the evening unfolding with flowers and a bonfire. As she gazed into the ceremonial flames, a new scene emerged.

Saman sat beyond the fire, watching her with his legs crossed. He glowed with a healing light. A green aura encircled him, and a sorrowful, strange melody of single notes played in the distance. The song moved closer, and from the shadows behind Saman, an old man emerged. He played a violin and had rough skin, a white beard, and short gray hair. He wore a red plaid shirt with a heavy chain wrapped around his waist. Thelma followed the chain to the woods behind the man. Between the trees, a large animal waited. *So strange, was it a bear? In Hawaii? A bear?*

As the man came forward, a brown bear did indeed step out of the woods, with the chain cuffed to its thick neck, walking on all fours. The man plucked the violin strings with his fingers, then dragged his bow across the instrument's neck. Saman didn't see the man or the bear behind him. Rather, he swayed to the music and watched the fire. The bear sat on its haunches like a dog.

Thelma decided the man was Saman's father. *But surely, he didn't have a pet bear in real life. Saman was musical, but had his father been musical?* Then, as abruptly as she had gained the vision, it disappeared. Behind her eyelids was only black space. *Damn, I lost my focus.* She sighed and pursed her lips. Sustaining and interpreting her visions was still a challenge. She'd extracted something from the meditation, but what did it mean?

HIS FOOT ON THE GAS, Saman sped down the tropical country road like a person fleeing the police. *Why do I act that way?* he wondered. *Why am I such a dick?* He gripped the Jeep's steering wheel to steady himself. He'd taken another Oxy when he'd gotten up, before going outside. *I probably shouldn't be driving,* he thought. *Where am I even going?* He drove towards the ocean, hoping it would offer a dramatic view. *Thelma didn't mean to hurt my feelings, but what she said is true. I'm a loser, a total loser.*

He passed a few rundown cement houses nestled in the banks of scrubby plants, and ferns. *I should turn around.* Still, the beautiful scenery propelled him to keep driving. He curved closer to the ocean and came to a small parking lot facing the sea.

Saman parked the Jeep and got out. The ocean smashed onto the rocks with a force unlike anything Saman had ever seen in Florida. *How could anyone swim in this?* he wondered. Despite the rough surf, two men stood near the water, with brown skin, baseball caps, and arms covered in tattoos. Each man held a string attached to a small wooden raft with a square white sail, no larger than a book — like a boat that a child might play with in a bathtub. Turbulent waves tossed the tiny boats and it amazed Saman that they weren't being smashed to bits on the rocks. *Weird,* he thought. One man noticed him. Saman waived. Neither man returned the gesture. They both glared at him, as if he was an intruder on the island. Uncomfortable, Saman turned his head to avoid their stares. His gaze landed on an unmanned wooden stall like a child's lemonade stand, with the words "*Hawaiian Honey*" hand-painted in faded yellow letters, in the grass under a shade tree beside the beach.

He walked over to the stand. A few jars of honey rested on the wood counter. "Hello," he called. Maybe he could get a jar of the honey for Thelma. It was the least he could do to make up for being a moody dick and she did like honey in her coffee. "Anyone here?" he asked louder.

No answer.

Saman reached for his wallet. *I'll leave a five on the counter*, he thought. His hand however met with empty fabric. *Shit.* In his haste to leave, he'd walked out without grabbing his wallet. The honey didn't have a brand label and there were only a few jars with Hawaiian fabric-covered lids. *This probably would help the rest of the day go smoother,* he thought, *a small token, but still something.* He glanced back at the ocean. The fishermen now had their backs to him. He grabbed a honey jar.

As he returned to the Jeep, he considered asking the men if they knew who sold the honey, but something about their rough exteriors made him hesitate. Instead, he shoved the glass jar in his pants pockets and jumped into the Jeep.

When he reached home, Thelma was in the bedroom putting on a yellow bikini. He wrapped his arms around her bare stomach and squeezed her from behind. Thelma didn't say anything but allowed him to press his body into hers. She smelled like sunblock and coffee. "I'm sorry I flew off the handle," he said, "but I found this while I was out. Didn't see any grocery stores though." He handed her the honey jar.

Her expression softened. "That's very sweet of you," she smiled, "no pun intended. But I'm serious, Saman, when we get home, you really need to do something about your anger. It isn't fair to me and it isn't healthy for you." She hugged him. "I want you to be happy."

He stiffened with guilt, but returned her embrace. She was right, but he didn't know what to do. He'd tried pills, therapy, and group counseling. Hell, he'd even gone to an acupuncturist. "I'm sorry," he murmured into Thelma's hair. He was lucky she wasn't madder. Despite his erratic behavior, she always remained calm. He admired her patience. "You're right. I'll get help. You're right," he repeated, still hugging her. "And listen, let's hike to those waterfalls after all."

"Thank you. I'd love that."

"Yeah, we can have our chill day tomorrow."

"Well, the mushroom ceremony is tomorrow, but before we leave, sure." She squeezed his hand. "I think the ceremony is going to help."

Shit. The mushroom ceremony. . . He'd forgotten about it. His heart rate increased. A spark of anxiety lit in his chest. Maria knew him well, and put him at ease, but he wouldn't know anyone here. Was a mushroom ceremony really what he needed? He'd still been taking the Oxy. *Surely it couldn't be good to mix the two...*

Before Saman could articulate his concerns, Thelma pointed to the bikini string encircling her torso. "Can you put sunblock on my back?" she asked with a flirtatious smile, passing him a squeeze container of lotion.

12

S aman and Thelma hiked a winding, packed-dirt trail to the edge of the Akaka Falls. The sky, heavy with clouds, sprinkled as they walked. Saman breathed in shallow gulps as he trudged up the incline. They'd pigged out on Hawaiian BBQ at a roadside restaurant, and now he was sluggish. *Man, I'm out of shape,* he thought.

A bamboo forest surrounded them, and purple and white orchids hung off moss along the trail. They reached a flight of narrow rock steps. Climbing the wet surface, Saman worried he might fall.

"Maybe we'll see a rainbow, with this weather," Thelma said, looking around in wonder.

"Yeah," was all he could get out of his mouth. *She's in much better shape than I am,* Saman thought.

Thelma reached the top and motioned for him to come faster. "Look," she said, pointing to something in the distance.

Saman finally reached the top step, out of breath, and leaned against the metal railing of the small observation deck. A strip of white cascaded into a valley of verdant green, but the waterfall was so far away that he could barely see it; the water was no wider than his index finger.

"That's it?" he said. "We hiked all this way for that?"

Thelma crinkled her nose. "I think it's beautiful." She took a picture of the falls with her camera.

"This doesn't look like the picture online. This can't be it. There must be another one," Saman said, annoyed they'd walked so far to see a tiny waterfall a mile away through the trees.

"I don't know," Thelma said, "I think this is it."

A group of what appeared to be university students passed by holding iPads and taking pictures, laughing and speaking to each other in animated German.

"Then where were all those kids going?" Saman asked. "We should follow them." He headed back on the trail. *Why must we get lost every time we go anywhere in Hawaii?* He wondered. He was almost ready for the trip to end. Hot and sweaty, his feet hurt in his sneakers.

After another ten minutes of walking, Saman's hunch proved correct. The path opened to a horseshoe-shaped ledge facing majestic white waterfalls. He exhaled, despite his negative attitude, the view of the falls stopped him mid-step. Chutes of water hurled down black rocks and jungle, maybe 10 or 15 stories high, then splashed into an emerald pool below. Saman and Thelma watched the falls from a paved overlook with a guard rail. All the German students posed for selfies and group pictures, and a rainbow swept over the valley, collecting colors in its mist.

"I'm so glad we came," Thelma said.

"Me too," Saman said. When the German students moved on, Saman took Thelma's hand and led her to the water's edge. He pointed to an information placard. "It's higher than Niagara Falls."

"Have you been to Niagara Falls?" Thelma asked. "It's a crowded mess with McDonalds and Starbucks and tacky casinos."

"I've never been."

Arm in arm, the couple took in the nature, the beauty, and the loud sounds of rushing water. They lapsed into silence, mesmerized by the scenery.

Eventually, another group of tourists came, and Thelma and Saman stepped out of the way, so the new visitors could take pictures in front of the landmark.

Saman went to walk back in the direction they'd come from, but Thelma stopped him. "What do you think is that way?" She pointed past the falls, to a narrower path leading into the jungle.

"I don't know."

"Let's see," Thelma said. On the trail, the tropical forest thickened, and they reached a metal bridge arched over a gurgling, rock-strewn creek. Slimy dark green moss coated the structure's surface.

"Is that safe?" Saman asked, skeptical.

"If it wasn't, wouldn't they have blocked it off?"

Before he could answer, Thelma strode onto the bridge. "Hey, I don't know if we should walk on that," he called after her.

"Oh, come on, it's fine." She grabbed the bridge's rails and shook them, then kept going.

As if that proves anything, Saman thought. Frustrated and hot, he followed her, paying attention to each step, not wanting to slide or slip. Feeling tired and light-headed, he tried not to look down.

Thelma, oblivious to any danger the long bridge posed, stopped and asked him, "So, are you excited about the ceremony tomorrow?"

Saman raised his eyebrows, "Not really, to be honest. And come on, let's get off this thing. Keep moving."

Thelma started walking again, but kept talking, "I sensed that. Why not?"

"I don't know. I'm ready to stop dragging our bags around every few days." He omitted that he was leery of the ceremony on account of the prescription opioids he'd eaten like popcorn during the trip.

Thelma slowed ahead of him. "Careful, it's really slippery here."

"Maybe we shouldn't do the ceremony?" Saman added, gripping the bridge's railing. "There are so many other things to see on this island. We could do a mushroom ceremony at home."

Thelma stared at him like he'd turned into a coconut tree. "I'm really excited about the ceremony. I think it's going to be great, and it will be a unique experience here that we can't repeat. It's more than a mushroom ceremony. He uses a special blend of plants that he grows himself here on the island. He calls it *psilohuasca*. It's like magic mushrooms mixed with part of the ayahuasca brew, the harmaline, which makes the mushroom trip more intense and longer lasting. We can't get that at home."

The words stuck like a needle. "*Part of the ayahuasca brew*" and "*more intense*"? That would be an even worse mix with the opioid. *Maybe I should just tell her about the pills*, but the idea filled him with dread. Thelma would think he was so weak and also irresponsible. *Plus, I don't actually have a problem with the pills. I have a problem with PTSD, and the Oxy helps.*

"Are you listening?" She stopped again on the bridge. "You're a million miles away lately."

"Please, let's get across this bridge," he snapped, irritated. "It's making me nervous to be on this old thing, like who knows if it's about to fall apart." They were a huge distance off the ground. He didn't even want to think about what would happen if they fell.

Thelma raised her eyebrows, "You're being paranoid, but okay."

"Well, I should be, the universe hasn't exactly been on my side lately," Saman shot back. "And you didn't tell me it was going to be psilohuasca or whatever it is. I'm not trying to throw up and how do I know that's going to be okay with my kidney meds?"

"After I confirmed we were coming, a nurse who helps with the ceremony emailed some stuff. I thought I forwarded it to you?" Thelma said.

"I didn't see it, and aren't we supposed to be on a special diet if it's like ayahuasca. We've been eating fish tacos and croissants all week. Is this really a good idea?"

"She said people rarely throw up. It's not exactly ayahuasca, it's different, easier on the body. She just said no heavy food or meat the day of the ceremony. I also already sent them your list of your medications, and they approved all your meds."

"Well, you should've told me."

"I sent you an email. Sorry, things were kind of busy for me with clients before we left."

"Still, you could have mentioned it to me."

"Sorry, you're right."

"Anyway, let's go. I really don't like being on this bridge."

She obliged him and they finally reached the bridge's end. Saman exhaled. He just wanted to get back to the car, to change into flip flops and return to the cube house, but instead they met another stone staircase leading up a steep hill.

"I'm surprised you don't want to go to the ceremony," Thelma said. "Maria spoke so highly of the guy hosting it and you're usually excited to do ceremonies with me."

Why wouldn't she leave this topic alone? Saman brushed a small, black bug off his face. "Like I said, I'm not feeling it this time, and with your eye, maybe it's not good to be taking weird drugs."

"It's not drugs," Thelma retorted, irritated. "It's plant medicine."

Saman shrugged, "Well, as I said, I don't want to go — like... I'm not in the mood for it."

Thelma locked eyes with him and squeezed his shoulder. "I'm not going to force you, but I really want us to go."

He averted her stare, "Maybe you go, and I'll stay and chill at the cube house."

Thelma shook her head. "This is our honeymoon. I don't want to go alone."

He sighed, "You say you want to know how I feel. Well, I'm telling you how I feel."

"Yes, but you think it'll be too much work, or you don't want to meet a bunch of new people, but I'm sensing the opposite. It'll be exactly what we need."

"You don't know that. I could relive the transplant." *Relive the transplant...* The words made his heart pound harder.

"Maybe you *need* to relive it to move on."

"Let's see how we feel tomorrow," he said, thinking, *maybe I'll pretend to be sick tomorrow.* "Does this trail loop back to the parking lot?" he wanted to change the subject. "If we're going to meet that doctor at sunset, we should head back."

"Everything will be okay. This ceremony will be the highlight of our trip." Thelma batted her lacy blue eyes, then climbed up the steps. Although sweat beaded across his forehead and his thigh muscles ached, he had no choice but to follow her.

BACK AT THE CUBE HOUSE, Saman switched out of his sweaty t-shirt and into a lightweight Hawaiian shirt that Thelma bought him as a gift in Oahu.

"Ooh, you look so handsome," Thelma said, slipping on a fresh, pale-pink sundress.

"You look beautiful too." He hugged her and kissed her lightly on the lips.

"With this eye? Really?"

He said yes to make her feel better, but she was right, her eye looked terrible. The bruise had deepened, and solid red replaced the white area. If not for her eye, he would have insisted they skip meeting the owners. Small talk was not his idea of fun and his leg muscles ached from the waterfall hike.

They made their way to the orange glow of the swimming pool and patio in front of the main house. A dense field of stars glimmered overhead, and a round white moon hovered in the distance over the black sea. Hawaiian ukulele music played from speakers mounted to the house's awning. Lit tiki torches marked the four corners of the pool, and exotic flowers in pinks and reds spilled out of cement planters along the patio's edge.

"Wow," Thelma breathed to Saman, "I can't believe people actually live here full-time, right on the ocean like this."

"I guess being a doctor is pretty good business," Saman replied.

No one was by the pool. The outdoor lights were on, but the inside was dark.

"Do you think they forgot?" Thelma asked.

"I hope not, for the sake of your eye," Saman said.

"I'll knock on the door."

A light switched on in the house and through the glass windows, a female silhouette moved. As Dan and the doctor came outside, Saman's eyes widened. The doctor was at least twenty years older than Dan, with gray hair in a bun. Saman tried to conceal his surprise. He glanced at Thelma; she looked unfazed by the mis-matched couple.

"Hello and welcome. I'm Roberta." The woman placed a tray of crackers, cheese, and fruit on the table, then extended her arms to hug Thelma and Saman. She wore an ivory sundress with a sheer shawl around her shoulders and looked more like an aging hippie than a wealthy doctor.

"We have wine and also some delicious guava juice, Hawaii's finest," Dan said.

"Thank you," Thelma exclaimed. "We aren't drinking tonight, we got carried away and had pretty bad hangovers recently, but the juice sounds wonderful."

"Dan tells me you hurt your eye?" Roberta squinted at Thelma in the dim outdoor lighting. "Let's go inside for a better look?"

Thelma nodded. "Yes, thank you so much, that would be great."

Dan put his arm on Saman's shoulder, "You and I can have a smoke while they do that? I've got some Maui-wowi." He pulled out a thick joint.

Saman agreed, some pot sounded amazing. That would probably help the soreness in his legs too. They settled onto sofas made from giant logs with overstuffed red cushions. Dan passed the joint and a lighter to Saman who inhaled the fragrant marijuana. As he handed it back to Dan, Saman started coughing. "Woah. That's strong."

Dan grinned. "So, how do you like Hawaii? You know I've never been to Florida, but I hear it's great."

Saman nodded. "You aren't missing much, compared to this." He gestured to the ocean.

Dan took a deep drag on the joint, held it in, then let out a stream of smoke. "Yeah, I love this place."

The doctor returned with Thelma now wearing a black eye-patch.

Saman stood. "How is her eye?"

"I'm sorry to say that I think she may have scratched her cornea or iris," the doctor answered. "The patch will help with the light sensitivity, but she should see an eye doctor."

Thelma looked deflated. Saman knew she was hoping the eye would heal with no intervention.

"I've written her a prescription for some drops as well, to ward off potential infection. You can fill it tomorrow. I gave Thelma the address of the pharmacy. It's not far."

"Thank you," Saman said. *Yes,* he thought, *now we definitely can't go to the ceremony.*

Roberta poured juice for Saman and Thelma while Dan smoked the joint down to a tiny stub between his fingers. He looked young enough to be Roberta's teenage son.

"How long have you lived here?" Thelma asked.

"Oh gosh," Roberta said, "for decades now."

Saman and Thelma listened as Roberta explained how she'd come to Hawaii after splitting from her husband. "Divorce was frowned upon back then, and I wanted to escape everyone's judgment. Eventually, I went to med school in Honolulu and later set up my practice here."

"That's amazing," Thelma said.

Saman realized he was really high. *Damn,* he thought, *I shouldn't have taken so many hits.*

"But you check out tomorrow? Not a long stay. Where do you go next?" the doctor asked.

Hopefully nowhere, Saman thought.

"We are going to visit a friend of a friend who has a place about an hour from here," Thelma replied.

"Wonderful," Roberta said.

Saman jumped in, "But maybe we won't go. Could we stay here if we wanted to extend our booking?"

Thelma shot Saman an annoyed look.

"For sure," Dan said, "we don't have anyone coming right after you. That would be great. I'll take you to the mermaid pond if you want?"

"That's very kind," Thelma interjected, "but we'll probably stay with our friend."

Saman lay his hand on Thelma's, but she moved hers away and picked up her glass of juice.

"The volcano park is good too," Dan added. "Don't miss that." He poured himself and Roberta more wine. "And like I said, the Green Beach is the only green beach in the world. Right, love?" He squeezed Roberta's leg. Saman shifted in his chair. *Why would this guy want to be with such an older lady? She must be in her late fifties*, he thought, *if not her sixties.*

"No, I think there are three or four others, but it's worth seeing. A rough ride to get there, though." She also poured a glass of wine.

"How did you guys meet?" Thelma asked.

Dan and Roberta looked at each other and laughed.

"Should we tell them?" Dan teased, rubbing Roberta's thigh.

Saman could not help but stare.

"Why not?" Roberta squeezed Dan's leg.

"We met at a nudist tantra retreat." He winked at Saman.

Saman almost spit out his juice.

"Oh!" Thelma's eyes bulged. "I was not expecting that answer!"

Roberta and Dan giggled. "Yes, it was an incredible retreat," Dan said through his laughter. "Life changing. We enjoy being nudists, but don't worry, when we have guests we keep it G-rated."

"Or maybe PG," Roberta added, and the two kissed.

Saman averted his eyes, feeling uncomfortable, though he wasn't sure why. It was just weird to see a man his age with a woman who looked as old as his mother. Then again, guys did this stuff all the time. *Maybe I'm being sexist,* he thought.

"That's wonderful," Thelma said.

"And what about you? How did you meet?" Dan asked.

"Um," Thelma paused.

Saman realized their story was almost as ridiculous. How could they laugh at this couple when they'd met at a plant medicine ceremony — it sounded equally flaky.

Thelma took the plunge. "We met at a retreat as well," Thelma said, "not a nudist retreat, but, um, a meditation retreat."

Dan and Roberta nodded, "Meditation, nice." Dan said. "Are you guys both into like yoga and stuff then? Wellness?"

Thelma smiled, "Yes, I try to meditate every day and I do yogic breathing. I find it really helps my creativity."

Saman wished they could go back to the cube house; he wanted to lay down.

As the evening wore on, Dan and Roberta finished the wine, then opened another bottle. They regaled Saman and

Thelma with stories of crazy past guests, local Hawaiian folklore, and their nudist adventures. Saman could hardly sit up straight. All the marijuana mixed with the pills he'd taken earlier, and the strain of the hike made him yearn for his bed.

When the second bottle of wine reached the halfway mark, Saman made his move. "Well, it's getting late, we should go to bed, but thank you so much for your hospitality." He rose from the sofa with some effort, his legs feeling like sandbags.

"Don't go now," Dan said, "the party's just getting started."

Roberta pinched him, "Let the lovebirds return to their nest!"

"Ah, come here you guys." Dan and Roberta gave them a big group hug. Saman tried to politely participate in the embrace, but he pulled away as soon as it seemed reasonable, feeling uncomfortable to have his body so close to strangers.

As they reached the cube house, a shriek followed by a loud splash came from the pool. Dan and Roberta had both stripped off their clothes and jumped into the water.

"Well, that was crazy," Saman said as they got inside and shut the glass door behind them.

"They're sweet," Thelma said. "I mean, kudos to her."

"Yeah, that's probably what you'll do after I die," Saman joked, tickling Thelma, "Bag yourself a hot, young Aussie."

"Never," Thelma said, slipping off her dress, "and you're not dying. When we get old, they're going to upload our brains and we'll live forever together in the cloud."

"You're already living in the clouds," Saman said, yawning and stripping off his clothes.

"Do they allow pirates in the clouds?" she pointed to the eye mask. "What do you think? Do I look sexy?"

"Very," Saman slid into bed.

Thelma snuggled under the covers, naked beside him. "I'm sleepy too," she yawned. "I wanted to have sex, but I'm too beat. That old doctor has more energy than we do."

"That weed did me in," Saman said, his eyes already closed.

"You shouldn't have even smoked it at all, with the ceremony tomorrow. It isn't good to put other substances in your system," she scolded him. "I actually couldn't believe it when I saw you smoking."

Instead of responding, he spooned Thelma's warm body, pressing himself to her naked bottom, his arm draped over her curved, soft hip and, in an instant, he was asleep.

A BEAM of pale moonlight seeped into the bedroom and the sound of a door cracking open stirred Saman awake. He tried to rub his eyes, but his arm was asleep. The sliver of light expanded. *Where was Thelma? Had she gone outside? But why?*

The door opened wider. *Was it car headlights?* They'd left their bedroom door open, giving him a direct line of sight to the front of the house.

He struggled to move his arms again. His limb felt detached. The more effort he exerted, the more his muscles refused to function. *What the fuck? Thelma!* He tried to say her name, but no words came. *Am I dreaming?* But no, he was awake. *Had he locked the door before going to bed?*

A shadow entered the house, temporarily blocking the light beam.

Who the fuck is here? He tried to shout, but couldn't.

Adrenaline went through him like a shotgun firing. *I need to wake Thelma.* A black silhouette moved through the living room. Saman used all his might to scream. His eyes felt heavy, blurry, his vision went in and out like someone had drugged him. *Did those nudist freaks poison us? Did that doctor put something in the juice? But why?* With great effort, he managed to heave his arm over to touch Thelma, but she didn't wake up.

The shadow of the man moved closer.

Get out! Saman wanted to shout.

Was it Dan in the doorway? What was he doing in here?

Terrified, Saman's breath accelerated in shallow gasps. *This weirdo is going to kill us,* he thought.

The figure stepped into the bedroom. Saman tried to writhe and jerk himself out of bed, to swing his legs, but he felt like an inert blob of jello. Panic seized his chest.

The man said nothing but strode with deliberate steps towards the bed. He was tall, but it was too dark to see his face; Saman couldn't tell if it was Dan or someone else.

He hyperventilated. Fear paralyzed him. *Thelma will wake up. She must wake up,* he thought. As if trying to communicate telepathically, he repeated in his mind, *"Thelma, wake up! Thelma, wake up!"*

Why can't I fucking move!?

The man stood over Saman, next to the bed. Saman quaked with fear. *I'm about to have a heart attack*, he thought. He tried to claw his way out of the paralysis that held him down like straps on a gurney. *They poisoned us. These nudist freaks poisoned us.*

The man reached into his pocket and pulled out a glimmering object. Moonlight reflected on the silver edge of a knife.

"Thelma," he screamed, and this time the words came

out, but garbled and strange. His lips felt numb, like after dental surgery. "Thelma!" He muttered again.

The intruder ignored him. In slow motion, the man stuck out his knife and cut a slit in the side of Saman's arm.

Pain erupted from the wound and spread through his shoulder. Saman screamed. The man covered Saman's mouth with a gloved hand. Saman's eyes went wide; the man had no face. The man kept cutting him in dull thrusts, moving from his arm to his torso, carving a hole in his chest.

"Help! Help me!" Saman screamed into the man's glove. Then terror overtook his mind, and the world went black.

13

Thelma leaned on a moss-covered log in a forest of wet leaves wearing cut-off jean shorts and a faded orange t-shirt. Mushrooms grew around her and Rhino, her younger brother's childhood dog, a broad-shouldered pit-bull mix, stood guard, monitoring the woods.

Strange, she thought, *that I should be here with Rhino. Where is my brother?*

The dog let out a bark.

"What is it?" she asked Rhino.

He barked again. She scratched his neck and he surveyed her with his all-knowing dog eyes.

The leaves rustled and the wind carried a tiny sound like a meowing cat.

"Did you hear that, boy?" Thelma rubbed the dog behind his ears. Rhino shook off her hand and trotted toward the sound.

"Rhino, come back," she called, but the animal disappeared into the pine trees.

The whimpering sound moved closer.

"Rhino," she called again. Rhino barked, then animal

screams came into her dream, louder and louder until she opened her eyes and sat up in bed.

Saman lay beside her crying in his sleep.

"Saman," she whispered

With his eyes closed, he moaned louder, then made a garbled screech like he was trying to scream.

"Saman," she touched at his arm.

He winced and mumbled something in Farsi, then rolled away from her, pulling the covers with him.

She sighed and got out of bed. In the bathroom, she sat on the toilet to pee. During Saman's nightmares, she never knew if she should wake him, or let him be. Her own dream made her miss her little brother. She hadn't seen him in years. He'd moved to Japan to work for a robotics company in Tokyo, and rarely came home, even skipping her wedding, claiming that he hated flying. She'd invited him to come visit them in Hawaii during the honeymoon, so he could meet Saman, but he'd declined.

Thelma finished peeing and splashed water on her face at the bathroom sink. The bruising on her face looked even more purple. She climbed back into bed. Saman snored lightly now, and she spooned him, then drifted off to sleep.

WITH A JERK, Saman flashed open his eyes. He was alone. "Thelma," he called, then examined his arm. It was in perfect condition. *What the fuck?* he thought. *Was it a dream?* The man with the knife had seemed so real.

"Hey, babe," Thelma said, appearing in the doorway in her bathing suit and a sheer white coverup.

Saman ran his fingers from his bicep to his wrist. "I..." He stopped, searching for the right words.

"You were talking in your sleep last night," Thelma said.

He ignored her, went to the front door and turned the handle: locked.

"Are you okay?" Thelma asked, following him.

He shook his head, confused. "I dreamed someone came into our room and I couldn't move. I thought I'd been poisoned." His heart still pounded with leftover adrenaline.

"You were in a deep sleep."

He leaned into her body and exhaled, stroking her hair like he was a little girl and she was his doll.

"Can I make you breakfast?" she finally said, rubbing Saman's arm. "I asked Dan if we could stay until noon, and he said that was fine."

"Yes, okay." After she left the room, he stared at the ceiling. *Fuck*, he thought. *You're in fucking paradise here, man, get a grip.* He slid shorts over his boney hips, and went to the kitchen, though his heart still pounded.

Thelma passed him a plate of cut pineapple and sweet rolls drizzled with honey. "I'm going for a quick dip in the pool before we check out," Thelma said.

"Hey, listen," Saman sat at the table. "I really don't want to do this ceremony tonight. I'm serious, and you need to see an eye doctor. Let's stay here for the rest of the trip."

"I called the optometrist this morning. He doesn't have any openings until after our flight home."

Fuck, why can't she cooperate with me?

"My eye is better this morning, anyway. Everything will be fine." She tried to sit on his lap, but he stiffened and shifted his body towards the table.

Should he escalate his objection or go along with her? The few times he'd done mushrooms before it had always been pleasant, but there was something in his mind screaming that this particular ceremony was a bad idea.

"If you truly don't want to go, we won't, but I can't pretend I won't be disappointed."

"I'm not in a good place, especially after last night. I thought someone had come into our room and was cutting me with a knife."

"They didn't cut you. It was a bad dream." She took his hand. "Please come with me."

He stared at his plate of food. *Maybe she was right?* While he felt like taking one of his pills and going back to sleep, something an older man in his group therapy said came to his mind — "Whenever you don't want to do something, it's usually what you need to do."

Thelma's single, un-patched blue eye waited for his answer, hopeful as a robin's egg. She was too beautiful and too determined. He couldn't say no. *I can go a few days without taking the pills,* he told himself. *It's not like I'm addicted. I just use them medicinally. Worse comes to worse,* he thought, *I'll pawn the mushrooms and sleep during the ceremony.* "Okay, you win. I'll come with you."

"Thank you," she said with a triumphant smile.

"But if anything bad happens," he added, "I'm blaming you."

She laughed, "Oh, God, don't say that."

ROCKY LAVA FIELDS morphed into lush rainforest as they drove from the sea to the interior of the Big Island of Hawaii.

"Is that from the erupting volcano?" Saman pointed to a plume of gray smoke in the distance.

"I think so," Thelma watched the trees zoom past the Jeep Wrangler's rolled-down window.

"That must be why there aren't many houses here; no one wants to live near a volcano."

"Except this Bāne Kama guy." Thelma's skin itched under the eyepatch from Roberta. It took all her willpower not to touch it. She pulled out her phone and read the text from Bāne Kama's assistant. It listed an address, a time, and some preparation instructions, like what to pack and what and when to eat before the ceremony. Thelma didn't know where they would sleep. *Did he have a guest bedroom? Or would they camp outside?* She only knew that Maria adored the man and she trusted Maria's judgment.

The road tapered, engulfed by dense foliage on both sides. Thelma's body tingled with excitement. Despite Saman's fears about the ceremony, she predicted a positive change on their horizon. Since beginning her journey with plant medicine, she'd learned to trust her instincts. Something was coming — a sign, a revelation, or maybe a powerful healing for Saman.

As they drove through a dark tunnel of trees arched over the road, she slipped a sweater over her thin, floral sundress. Sliding the brown cabled-yarn cardigan over both arms, she winced. She hadn't escaped getting a Hawaiian sunburn, despite her best efforts. *Hopefully it will turn into a tan instead of peeling,* she thought.

"You cold?" Saman asked. "We can put the top up."

"No, I like it down. I'm fine." She closed her eyes as Saman drove and let her mind drift back to the dream she'd had of her brother's dog, Rhino. Like the pit bull, she wanted to be Saman's protector, to shield him from harm, to be a watchful companion, sensing what was to come, and scouting ahead for threats or rewards. *That is what a wife should do,* she thought. *Or was it a presumptuous idea?* No, it was her truth. While it was more of a stereotypical male role to serve and protect, this was what she'd always wanted from every relationship, the opportunity to care for someone, to keep them safe. *Was she doing that now? Would this ceremony help her husband?*

The dream also made her miss her little brother. She'd invited him to come visit them in Hawaii during the honeymoon, so he could meet Saman, but he'd declined.

Turning to Saman, she said, "When I was a kid, my brother and I played this game called *The Wandering Druids.* Have you played it?"

Saman shook his head. "We only played Backgammon."

"Random," Thelma said, "I don't think I've ever played that."

"That's the only game I ever see Persians playing. But what were you saying? *The Wandering Clues*? What?"

She laughed, "No, *The Wandering Druids*. It was a board game with figurines and strategic missions. Everyone played a character. You had The Warrior- who was like Rambo, strong but lacking in wisdom. There was The Wizard, full of knowledge and spells, but physically weak. My mom always chose The Wizard. The Ranger could find hidden doors, read maps, and hunt for treasure chests, and The Blacksmith could build things and make weapons. Then there was a ghost who moved invisibly.

"So, what position did you play?"

"The Ranger, because I loved interpreting the maps."

"I can see you doing that."

"Yeah, and my brother always wanted to be The Blacksmith. He wanted to build things, hence working for the robotics company. No one ever wanted to be The Warrior."

"Your parents needed a third kid," Saman grinned.

Thelma smiled. "We actually joked that we wished Rhino could read to play the extra character."

"That was your brother's pit bull?"

"Yes, actually that's what made me think of this. I had a dream about him last night."

"I always wanted a dog, but my mom never allowed it." Saman frowned.

"Which character would you have played?" Thelma asked.

"Oh, I don't know. Wizard sounds good. But really, I'm not into games, never was."

"But you like video games."

"Oh yeah, I always loved video games, but my parents would never buy the system, so I had to play at friends' houses."

"What was your favorite video game?"

"Why are you asking me this stuff?"

"I'm curious. You don't talk that much about your childhood."

"Probably *Manic Killer*, pretty normal adolescent boy stuff."

Thelma nodded. "What about musical instruments? Did your parents play any instruments?"

"What? Now you're really asking some random questions. No, they didn't. Sorry to disappoint you — but my family wasn't as sophisticated as yours. We didn't play games or musical instruments. There were no intellectual group activities."

Thelma hadn't meant for the question to highlight their class differences, though now she saw it did. Saman's dad worked as a taxi driver before he died, while her father was still a University professor. "Maybe one day we can play the games with our kids," she offered. "I love Scrabble and Chess too."

"Now you're really talking crazy. I don't want kids

anytime soon."

"Well, we can't wait too long. I'm not getting any younger and neither are you." She squeezed his thigh.

Saman scrunched his face, "You're in a weird mood."

"Is it weird? I don't know. Maybe because our honeymoon is almost over, and real life will start too soon. I'm feeling nostalgic already."

"Real life would really start if we had kids. Plus, we can't afford a kid right now," Saman gripped the steering wheel.

"Yeah, of course. No, I wasn't saying right this second," she sighed. Did her desire to protect Saman stem from some unfulfilled maternal instinct? The more time she spent with Saman's little niece, Suri, the more she did want a child of their own.

"Good, because changing diapers isn't part of my current life plan," Saman added.

"What is your life plan then? Are you going back to school? You never talk about that anymore." Thelma folded her hands on her lap.

"My plan is to not get lost in Hawaii for the 100th time on this trip," he furrowed his brow.

They lapsed into silence. The winding road turned from pavement, to gravel, to dirt. Two vehicles followed them, a pickup truck and another Jeep.

"They must be headed to the ceremony too," Thelma said.

"I'm amazed they've even built roads here." Trees and brush scraped the sides of the Jeep.

Thelma checked her phone. "We have another mile." The small dot moved on her GPS until it stopped at an even narrower dirt route with grass growing between tire tracks.

Saman's cellphone rang in the cup holder.

"Who is that?" he asked.

Thelma picked up his phone. "It's an unknown number."

"Don't answer it."

"Are you sure?"

"Probably a robocall for health insurance." Saman wiped sweat off his face.

"Are you okay?" She placed the phone back in the cup holder.

It rang again, this time with a business name. "It's the lawyer," Thelma said. *Please let this be good news*, she thought.

"Okay, answer it."

Thelma accepted the call.

"Hello, this is Walter from Berkheimer and Clark. I'm calling for Saman Mohsen."

"Yes, he's right here." She put the phone on speaker mode.

"Hello," Saman said.

"Sorry to bother you on the weekend, but I've been trying to reach you, and I had emailed," the lawyer said.

Thelma's breath caught in her chest. Maybe the settlement was going through.

"Yes, sorry. We've been traveling," Saman replied.

"The anesthesiologist's insurance will settle your claim with the full sum allowed for these types of incidents. I need you to sign off on the documents. I've emailed them to you."

Thelma exhaled.

Saman responded, "What is that settlement amount?"

"It is $250,000, which is quite good for a case like this. I'd advise you to take the offer. If any new symptoms develop, we could revisit a personal injury suit, but for now this is the best outcome we could expect."

Thelma squeezed Saman's knee. She could barely

contain her excitement. It was not what Saman deserved. He deserved more, but it was something, some justice and closure for him.

"I guess, accept it," Saman said, "if you think that's the best we can do."

"I do. Great. Please sign the documents and send them back to me as soon as possible."

They finished the call.

Thelma grinned and laughed. "Wow! $250,000!" They could pay off their mortgage. Some of the money could be spent on therapy for Saman.

"Yeah, I'll believe it when I see the money," he said.

"We can do so much with that money. Babe, I'm so happy for you." Thelma leaned over the center consul and kissed Saman on the cheek.

"Probably after the legal fees and the taxes, we won't have much."

Thelma's face fell. Why couldn't Saman be happy for once? "He said it's a really good outcome."

"Yeah, good for him. He doesn't have to go to court and still gets paid," Saman shook his head, "and I live with nightmares."

Thelma put her hand on Saman's thigh. "Babe, you will get better."

"These assholes cheat everyone."

Thelma moved her hand back to her lap. There was no use talking to him.

"Maybe we shouldn't take it and fight these bastards in court."

"But you told him to accept it."

"Yeah, but I haven't signed anything."

"So, you want to get a second opinion or..."

"I don't really want to talk about it right now." Saman wiped sweat again off his forehead.

"You're really sweating."

"It's hot."

The GPS voice announced they had reached their destination — a steep dirt trail.

"This must be the driveway." Saman steered the Jeep down the verdant path. The vehicles behind them did the same. Thelma rolled up the Jeep's window to keep out the dust from their caravan of SUVs, driving through the bush, winding around massive trees and black rocks sticking out of the hillside.

"Man, if I lived here, I'd never leave," Saman said, "it would take too long to get anywhere."

The jungle parted to reveal a field and a sprawling modern estate. Parked cars dotted the grass. Thelma gasped. It resembled a tropical resort, not a regular person's house. An infinity edge pool flowed in front of the property like a horizontal waterfall. Towering palms and fruiting mango trees grew around the front yard. Solar panels covered the roof. Stone steps and a series of flower-covered terraces led to a large patio, strewn with outdoor sofas and tables. To the left of the pool, a path connected to a series of smaller A-frame guest houses.

"Wow!" Saman said. "What does this guy do again?"

"I don't know. I never asked Maria." Thelma raised her eyebrows. "Whatever it is, it must be lucrative."

The other guests pulled sleeping bags and suitcases out of their vehicles. Thelma and Saman did the same, following the stone steps to the swimming pool. The air smelled sweet with the fragrance of hibiscus and plumeria flowers. Young women with tan skin chatted to each other on the terrace, lounging in bikinis. A tall, thin woman in a short white dress, with blond hair like Thelma's, carried elegant glass pitchers of water on a silver tray. Thelma felt like she was in Beverly Hills in the 1970's, at a decadent Hollywood party. As they reached the upper level of the patio, she spotted a man behind the pool watching her with his arms crossed. Thelma's heart rate sped up. *Was the man Bāne Kama?* She grabbed Saman's hand.

The man moved toward them and locked eyes with Thelma.

She glanced away. "Saman," she whispered, "Do you see that man in the house watching everyone? I think he must be Bāne Kama."

Saman squinted. "I didn't see him. Where should we go?"

"I don't know." Thelma looked where the man had been, but he was gone. They wandered to the top of the pool and waited with their bags.

"Well, it seems like we're in good hands, judging by the looks of this place," Saman whispered, leaning over, his hot breath on her ear.

"Yes, it's really nice," she exhaled, glad the opulence was making Saman more comfortable. It had the opposite effect on her. This was nothing like the rustic, outdoor ceremonies she attended on the edge of the Everglades in Florida with mostly Colombian families. Saman was the only person of color at the pool. Everyone else was white. "Do you think we should go inside and look for the owner?"

"Sure," Saman nodded, picking up their bags.

Through open, floor-to-ceiling glass doors, the couple walked into an equally opulent living room. A few patrons sat on sofas and the ceiling was lined with teak wood. Abstract art and traditional Hawaiian carvings hung on the walls. They stood awkwardly in the center of the room. As

Thelma debated messaging the assistant, a warm hand touched her shoulder. It was the same tall man she'd locked eyes with. He put his other hand on Saman's shoulder, wedging himself between them. "I don't know you two, and I know everyone on this island," the man said. "So, you must be Thelma and Saman."

"Yep," Saman said, "That's us."

"Nice to meet you. I'm Bāne Kama." He shook Saman's hand first, then Thelma's. As the flesh of their palms connected, a flash of recognition struck Thelma. Her breath caught in her throat. She knew this man from somewhere, but where?

"Thanks so much for having us," Thelma said, still taken aback by a feeling of *déjà vu*. Bāne Kama looked like a Mr. Universe contestant and wore a tight pair of black bathing shorts that exposed his enormous thighs. His black hair was shaved short. A palm-sized wooden hook hung from a thick rope around his neck. Polynesian tattoos, black winding triangles, waves, and spears circled his swelling biceps. Even his face bore small, geometric designs in the corners and on his temples. But beyond his incredible height and fitness level, what shocked Thelma the most, was that he wasn't Hawaiian; he was a white guy with a dark tan.

"We were just trying to figure out where to go, Mr. Kama," Saman said.

Bāne Kama laughed, "Ah, y'all can call me Bāne."

Thelma's lips parted reflexively. Not only was he not Hawaiian, but he spoke with a southern accent, like he was from rural Georgia or Alabama.

Bāne winked at her. "Y'all make yourselves at home. Any friend of Maria's is a friend of mine. I've got you in the main house with me, in a room with a hell of a vista. You can settle in and then come back to the pool. We'll start in an hour, and no cell phones. Leave them in the house on silent, or better yet, turn them off."

His voice was familiar too. Had she heard him on TV? Thelma struggled to take in Bāne Kama's football-player size and his deep-south accent. "Thank you so much. We really appreciate it," she murmured.

"My pleasure," Bāne grinned, revealing perfect, white teeth. "Follow me." He touched Thelma's shoulder again. From his hand, energy, tingling, warm, and unexpectedly intense circulated down her body. Something about him made her very nervous. Buzzing with excess sensations, she glanced at Saman. He was oblivious to her reaction.

Bāne led them to a hallway of doors. Thelma tried to calm herself, looking at her feet as they walked, instead of at Bāne's impressive backside.

He opened the door to a room with varnished teak floors and silk wallpaper with silver orchids. Pillows with bold, Hawaiian tribal designs dotted a four-poster mahogany king-sized bed.

"Your home is incredible," Saman said.

"I try." Bāne saluted them, then left.

"Holy shit, this place is insane," Saman commented, flopping on the bed.

Thelma let out a breath and shook her head. "His voice sounds really familiar to me, like I know him from somewhere."

"Definitely not a Hawaiian accent, that's for sure."

She opened the room's curtains, revealing an expanse of green landscape stretched out to the endless cobalt Pacific.

"Forget the mushrooms," Saman said. "I'll stay right here with this view." He grabbed Thelma and wrapped his arms around her waist, burrowing his face into her hair and kissing her neck.

Already spun up and wanting to cool off, she pulled away. "Hey, our *Kundalini* energy is rising. We shouldn't get turned on before the ceremony."

"Shhhh." He put his finger over her lips. "Don't talk."

She let him slide his pointer finger between her lips, and she sucked on it, then he kissed her neck, but she was distracted by her desire to rush back to the swimming pool. She wanted to examine Bāne Kama again, to determine how she knew him. Surely, she would recall meeting such a large man, with so many tattoos. *I should have googled his name,* she thought. Her physical body had interpreted Bāne with a primal impulse, not as a predator, but as a desirable mate. She stifled the idea. It was too soon after her wedding to be attracted to another man. *It's his size,* she rationalized. *He probably makes every menstruating woman on earth feel that way.*

She pulled Saman's finger out of her mouth. "Okay babe, slow down. I need to focus, and I want to change before the ceremony."

"Okay, okay," Saman said, "You're right, and I should find my flashlight."

"Yes, good idea. I've got extra batteries if you need them." She hoisted her suitcase onto a luggage stand nearby. Pulling out her ceremony clothes, Thelma's mind swirled with anticipation. But now wasn't the time to build up expectations. She'd learned not to begin ceremonies with preconceived notions.

14

The afternoon sun glowed orange through a sprawling banyan tree bordering Bāne's patio. Participants clustered around the swimming pool holding bookbags, light jackets, and blankets for when night fell and the temperature dropped. As Thelma and Saman stepped out of the main house, a familiar voice called to them, "Well, bugger me!"

Thelma's jaw dropped like a drawbridge at the sight of Dan skipping towards them.

The young Australian hugged her. "Didn't expect to see you two today! You never said your friend was Bāne Kama!" Dan's denim-blue eyes gleamed.

Saman stammered, "Yes, um sorry. We didn't know you'd be here, either."

Dan hugged Thelma and Saman like they were his long-lost pals. "Bāne really does know everyone on this island."

What were the chances of seeing Dan again? Thelma wondered. She couldn't believe he was attending the same ceremony. The Big Island really was a small island.

"Is your girlfriend here too?" Saman asked.

"Roberta was supposed to come, but she got called last minute to assist with a baby delivery for a friend's daughter."

"Oh wow," Thelma responded, feeling a tad uncomfortable that she'd gone to the ceremony instead of following Roberta's orders to see the ophthalmologist.

"That's cool that Roberta comes to these," Saman said.

"Oh yeah, she really enjoys them," Dan said. "She was bummed she couldn't come tonight, but duty calls, you know."

Saman nodded.

Thelma could see Dan's words put Saman at ease. *Good*, she thought, *now he can relax knowing that Bāne's plant medicine is doctor-approved.*

"Have you done one of these ceremonies before?" Dan asked.

"Yes, in Florida, but with mushrooms, not psilohuasca. Is it pretty similar to regular mushrooms?" Thelma squinted in the sun.

"It's similar, but it lasts longer. I prefer it. Plus, Bāne's a master host. Come on, I'll take you round the pool and introduce you to everyone."

As Dan walked them around the patio like show ponies, Thelma and Saman exchanged bemused expressions. Everyone hugged and greeted them. Most guests were in their forties, but there were a few younger folks, including the college-aged children of some of the attendees.

Hawaiian men carrying gourd drums, guitars, ukuleles, and a large mallet instrument like a xylophone crossed the patio, heading to the woods behind the house.

"Ooh, I didn't know there was going to be live music," Saman said and squeezed her hand. "Sorry I was being so fickle about coming."

"It's okay. I'm just glad we're together." She gave him a quick kiss.

As their lips parted, a hush fell over the crowd and Bāne Kama strolled out from the living room. Bare-chested, he wore white linen pants with a belt of braided plant fibers and a necklace of golf-ball-sized black beads with a large Hawaiian fishhook dangling above his navel.

As he passed, Thelma got a better view of his tattoos, including a detailed drawing of an octopus on his spinal column, with tentacles wrapping around his sides, creating the effect of the creature riding on his back. He faced the crowd with his arms outstretched and palms lifted. The ocean shimmered in the distance beyond his sculpted physique.

Nervous energy sparked through Thelma and she shifted her legs to release the tension. Bāne opened his mouth and, in a deep, clear voice, bellowed a melody of fluid Hawaiian words.

Who was this man? The more Thelma saw him, the more she grew convinced that they'd met before.

The song finished and the audience applauded. Bāne pressed his enormous hands together in prayer and tipped his head. He scanned the crowd. "We'll now hike to the sacred ceremony space and begin our journey."

With the rest of the guests, they trailed behind Bāne's hulking form as he led them around the guest houses and up a hill; via a stone path, they entered the jungle.

Thelma could hear Saman's heavy breath, and after walking for about thirty minutes on the steep, rock-strewn trail, she also needed a break. Finally, they reached a grass clearing with a fire pit and a wooden, circular pavilion. The Hawaiian musicians arranged their instruments under the structure's thatched roof.

Bāne pointed to the building, "Leave anything you don't need under the *maloca*. Grab a mat and bring them around the fire circle. Let's experience this magnificent sun."

The mats were bright red and made of thick foam. Thelma and Saman positioned theirs next to each other, facing east. Beside the fire was a flat, gray rock, the size of a double bed. Dan waived to them from across the circle.

When they were all settled, Bāne Kama brought a large conch shell to his lips and blew it three times, making loud sounds like a foghorn. "The ceremony is now open! I welcome positive energy and beneficial blessings from the universe and all its forces. From this point on, please do not speak until I blow the shell again and close the ceremony." The audience listened in rapture.

Excitement moved like a flame on dry leaves through Thelma. She focused her mind. Maria always guided her to keep her intentions clear, but open and vague, rather than specific, with self-awareness, but without the assumption that she knew better than *The Divine*.

Her first instinct was to ask for things that were actually about Saman and not herself, but she knew this was misguided. Instead, she concentrated on releasing her desire to control external outcomes. She found herself also watching Bāne Kama. With his size and tattoos, it was hard not to stare.

Standing inside the circle, Bāne pointed to some young women wearing ankle-length white sundresses and lingering by the maloca. "Anais, River, and Sunita will light our sacred fire." He said. The three women came to him, carrying silver platters covered with kindling and flowers.

Thelma marveled at the beautiful figures. Their simple white dresses with green grass belts like Bāne's gave them a mythical quality.

As if reading Thelma's mind, Bāne spoke, "These women will serve as the three muses of our ceremony. Anais, come forward."

The girl who must be Anais approached the stone and Bāne slipped a Hawaiian lei around her neck. Instead of flowers, it was made of green fruit, like tiny limes, nestled amongst pink berries and leaves.

"You, Anais, are *Aoide*, our muse of song," Bāne said, adjusting the lei. "As the medicine moves within us, Aoide will gift us with her voice. If you feel lost or distraught during the ceremony, find yourself in her melodies."

Aoide took her place beside Bāne. Then he called the next woman and hung a lei around her neck. "Sunita, you are *Mneme* — the muse of memory. You watch over us, holding our experiences to recall any eventful happenings during our final integration tomorrow." Likewise, the muse of memory fell into line beside the muse of song.

"And finally, River." Bāne motioned to the blond woman who resembled Thelma. "River, you are *Melete,* our muse of care and attention. If anyone has a logistical or medical problem during the ceremony, find Melete and she will help you."

The muse of song struck a long match and lit a sage smudge; she wound it around the ceremony space, then used it to start the fire. Bāne stoked and blew on the flames until they spread to the overarching pyramid of logs. Then the muses offered trays of flowers to the guests. Each taking a palmful, Thelma, Saman, and the others arranged the fragrant pink and white petals around the stone circle.

"Bathrooms are over there," Bāne waved to a row of wood stalls. "If you need to go, go now." A few guests got up. The muses brought out another tray, this one laden with chocolates wrapped in wax paper.

Bāne stood. "Now, for those who have never sat ceremony with us, let me explain what will happen. You'll take
one chocolate on the first round. Then in an hour, I'll call
you to eat two more chocolates. After the next hour, you'll
take the last chocolate. Then an hour later, you'll meet
God." He chuckled and the audience laughed.

"For those of you that seek something beyond pleasure,
after everyone gets their last chocolate, you may eat more
until they're gone, but eventually, I'll remove the sacraments
so we can end our experience before dawn."

He held a chocolate in the air. "Please keep all your
wrappers and bring your trash with you at the end of the
ceremony. I'm not your shaman or your janitor. I'm just the
provider of this event. If you need to make noise, go away
from the group, but stay in the clearing." He gestured to the
woods. "There are wild pigs, and holes you can fall in. Don't
wander off."

As Thelma listened, Bāne locked eyes with her.

"Now," he said, "let's begin. Thelma, please start our
ceremony with the first mushroom offering."

She glanced around, startled.

"Yes, you, Thelma," Bāne repeated.

Embarrassed, she hoisted herself off the ground.
Everyone watched as she made her way to Bāne.

"Thelma is our special guest, from Florida," Bāne said,
"brought here by a dear friend of mine." He smiled at
Thelma and took her hands in his.

Surprised by his touch and words, her body went rigid.
She didn't know what to say. His large hands felt calloused
on her skin. She held her breath and her heart pounded.

Bāne leaned forward and spoke softly so that only she
could hear, "Are you ready for this?" He asked.

She couldn't answer. Heat rose on her cheeks and blood

rushed to her extremities. The space between their palms vibrated with awareness. *What did Maria tell him about me?*

"Please form a line behind Thelma," Bāne said.

Sweat dripped from Thelma's armpits. *Four chocolates,* she thought, *how much was in each?* That was a lot of psilohuasca. *How would Saman react to a high dose?* Likewise, she'd never eaten this much at once, unless they each only contained a small amount. She wished she'd asked Dan how much was in the chocolates. Her excitement turned to apprehension. *Maybe I shouldn't have pressured Saman to come*, she thought.

Bāne put both hands on her shoulders. Again, the heat from his palms transferred like blood into her veins. Her nipples hardened under her sundress and sweat collected between her breasts. His touch was something inhuman and powerful, otherworldly. She couldn't mentally control her physical reactions.

He tilted his forehead to hers. His breath felt warm on her lips. *What the hell is he doing?* she thought. She wanted to turn away. For a second, she felt faint. The sun, the fire, his breathing; it was too much. *No,* she thought. *Stop. This isn't right.* She didn't want this feeling. *He shouldn't be touching me like this.* But the smell of his sweat, the distance between his bare chest and her skin, it was activating something primal inside her. Just as she was unable to take any more, he stepped away.

"Take a chocolate," Bāne said with a smile. One of the muses stood beside him holding the tray.

Thelma picked one, then staggered back to her mat on the other side of the fire, in a daze, full of a kinetic force that Bāne had somehow deposited into her core. She resented him for having such a physical effect on her.

The chocolate was molded into the design of an eye. In

the heat, it melted between her fingertips. She slipped the morsel of sugar, cocoa, and mushrooms into her mouth. It tasted sweet, but also earthy and buttery, like roasted almonds.

Saman unwrapped and ate his own chocolate. *Had Bāne's energy also affected him?* Thelma wondered. *Was he feeling the same thing in a masculine way?* But she couldn't ask him. They were only allowed to speak to the muses during the ceremony.

"See you on the other side," Bāne said after the last person had taken their medicine. Then he popped a chocolate into his mouth. He moved his body into a seated yoga pose, his feet atop crisscrossed legs and his eyes closed, forming *mudras* or small o's on his thighs between his thumb and pointer finger.

Thelma shifted on her mat, lying on her back, then on her side. She checked on Saman; he lay with his eyes closed beside her.

Stop worrying about other people and connect with yourself, she thought.

Bāne soon called her for the second round of the mushroom chocolates. As Thelma stood, the world sparkled. The green grass shimmered as if covered in dew. This time she held Saman's hand and walked with him. Bāne did not touch Thelma, but stared past her like she was invisible.

The men under the maloca played rhythmic and entrancing music. The ceremony goers lounged and danced around the circle. Time was an elastic band, stretching until it snapped. A shimmering tapestry of colors painted the trees and wove together like threads on a loom. Thelma breathed in the smell of grass.

Next to her, Saman pulled up his blanket. She touched him and he gave her a thumbs-up.

He's okay, she thought, *my love, Saman, my husband, Saman.* His name echoed and split into hummingbirds. The jewel-eyed birds blinked, then multiplied and flew away.

A warm hand touched her leg. Thelma opened her eyes. Kneeling in front of her, Bāne held out a fourth chocolate. She ate it and licked around the paper's edges, then sucked the melted chocolate off her fingers. The psilohuasca designed a psychedelic dream, submerging her; she sank into its geometry.

15

W*hat should my intention be for this ceremony?* Saman wondered. He'd been so worried about the ceremony that he hadn't taken time to focus on a positive intention. Diamonds and triangles, intricate pyramids, undulated and superimposed over Saman's thoughts and vision, turning the forest into a scaffolding of fading greens and golds. He studied the patterns with awe until Bāne blocked his view.

The hulking man crouched with another silver tray of psilohuasca, the third round. Saman chose an eye-shaped chocolate. It tasted like hot cocoa and honey. He sucked on it until it covered every surface of his mouth with the sweet taste. Remembering the Hawaiian honey from the stall by the beach, he wondered if they'd used the same honey to sweeten the chocolates, instead of sugar? The fact that he'd stolen that honey troubled him a little. *It wasn't really okay, was it? No,* he answered himself. *Why did I do that?* But he didn't know, other than he'd acted stingy, or *was it selfish? Maybe lazy too?* It wasn't like him to be dishonest, *or was it?*

The question stung in his stomach as he swallowed the rest of the mushroom chocolate.

Perhaps my intention for this ceremony should be honesty... he thought, *or generosity?* That was one thing he liked about the Islam he knew from childhood — its emphasis on giving to charity, called *Zakat*, one of the five pillars of Islam. *Zakat* was a donation of 2.5% of your income annually to the needy, either directly or through a charity. *I haven't paid Zakat in years,* Saman thought. Then again, he was in debt now. *Weren't people in debt supposed to receive Zakat?* Though in Islam loans with interest were forbidden, so no one would be in this kind of debt. *Why am I thinking of this right now? I should be more generous.* Still, the world wasn't too generous to him, every time he tried to get ahead, things went wrong.

Saman glanced at Thelma, laying on her mat with her eyes closed and a serene expression on her sun-kissed cheeks. Unlike his wife, he disliked being on the ground. It felt like things were poking him, like he didn't have enough body fat to cushion himself from twigs or rocks. *I'm like the princess and the pea, except the prince version*, he thought and frowned. *What kind of man was he that twigs bothered him? I need to gain weight. I'm getting too skinny*. He stared at his hands and his bony kneecaps, they looked so old. Negative thoughts attached like leaches to his trip, sucking out the joy of the ceremony. *Maybe I need to eat more chocolates? Yes, I'm not tripping hard enough to stop my hamster-wheel brain from turning.*

He leaned forward, preparing himself to get up. *I'll go to the bathroom, and then eat more chocolates*. As he stood, his stomach churned, and his lower intestines gurgled. In the fire, he saw the shapes of lizards and burnt wood that resembled reptilian scales. His gut clenched and he felt dizzy from the heat. As fast as he could, he made his way to a port-a-john and dumped out the contents of his bowels into the hole below. As he released his lunch, it felt like the entire structure was shaking. Unsteady, he cleaned himself off with baby wipes. *Get me out of here,* he thought.

In the fresh air with an empty stomach, he felt slightly better, but his mind was still running like a broken sink. Before returning to his mat, he went to Bāne, who sat cross-legged like a Buddha on the large rock by the fire.

"Could I have another chocolate?" Saman whispered.

Bāne nodded and gestured to a small cooler resting against the rock in the grass.

Saman opened the cooler and plucked a wrapped chocolate. *Was one enough? Or should I take two*? Many chocolates remained. His stomach was calmed now, but his thoughts were still stuck in reality, like weeds needing to be yanked out of a flowerbed. *Time to go all the way,* he decided, surprising himself. *You're ready.* He took a second chocolate, then he returned to his mat and ate them both. *That was the third and fourth*, he noted. *Or was it the fourth and fifth? No, it couldn't be.* If each chocolate had one gram of psilocybin, which was his suspicion, then this was still only four grams, a substantial dose, but a reasonable amount, nothing too crazy. Some people he knew, like Maria and her husband, would eat eight grams in one sitting.

Taking a swig of his water, he covered his mat with his sleeping bag and lowered his lean body flat.

I still don't have an intention. I need one. More comfortable now, his body relaxed, and he slipped deeper into the trip.

Show me the future, he thought. *That will be my intention, prepare me for the future. Show me my next step in life.* He closed his eyes and focused on the idea.

But instead of the future, the mushrooms returned him to the past, to a time of disruption and change.

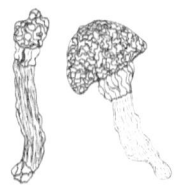

THE LIGHTS in the club made the stage floor glow blue. Saman worked beside one of the jazz venue's employees, a burly young Hawaiian man with a thick, black beard named Duke. They were setting up the PA system. *Wow, I forgot about Duke*, Saman thought, half-awake in the present in Bāne's circle and half in the past. Was he remembering him because of Hawaii? They'd been good friends, always drinking and hanging out late after shows. *Where was Duke now? I should try and get in touch with him*, Saman thought.

He returned to the memory and stayed there, enjoying the nostalgic feeling. Tonight, the *Skyland Trio* would play for a sold-out crowd in *Yoshi's*, Oakland, California's jazz and sushi joint. Saman had only been in the Bay Area for a few months, but he loved it there, the Japanese and Chinese food, the craft beer, and the live music, the buzz of the tech industry and the ever-changing, but never-too-cold weather.

"Pass me that adaptor," Duke said, pointing to a pile of plugs and cables near Saman's leather work boot-covered feet.

Saman crouched to get the cable and as he did, he felt an odd sensation in his legs, like they'd expanded in his jeans and were pressing against the seams of the denim. Surprised, he looked at his pants and his thighs did seem bigger. His jeans felt tighter. He stood quickly, alarmed by the sensation. *Maybe, I need to cut back on all the late-night noodles.* Duke was fond of a tiny place near the UC Berkeley campus, where they'd slurp huge bowls of *ramen* with thick slices of fat-rimmed pork.

"The adapter?" Duke repeated. "Did you just touch it and not pick it up? You high or what?"

Saman shook his head, "No, sorry."

He squatted down again, but with all his body weight on his knees and thighs, pain hit him. His legs suddenly felt like water-filled balloons ready to pop.

Something is wrong, he thought. Apprehension flooded his brain. He handed the cable to Duke, who gave him a puzzled frown. "You okay?" Duke asked. "You've got a weird look on your face."

Saman shook his head, "And you've got a weird looking face."

Duke laughed.

Saman turned away, his heart pounding. *Was this a hangover symptom?* He felt really bloated. "I'll be right back," he mumbled, then headed for the club's bathroom. He needed to examine his legs. As he walked, his limbs felt unusually stiff.

Inside the men's room stall he tried to slide off his jeans. Normally and easy task, he could hardly get them past his thighs. He stared, wide-eyed at his tan, hair-covered legs. Panic rang through his chest; his lower half was blown up like a balloon. *Oh, my God,* he thought, *I look like elephant man.* Almost dizzy, he wanted to sit on the toilet but feared it would hurt his legs or burst them. *What the fuck? I need to get to a doctor. Or maybe I'm dehydrated?* He painfully squeezed back into his pants and went to the bathroom sink. His face in the mirror was puffy too. Heart pounding, he returned to the stage.

"Uh... can you finish this setup?" He asked Duke. "I think I need to go to a doctor, like right now. Something's wrong with my legs."

Duke stopped what he was doing. "Really?"

"I'm swollen, I don't know. I think I need to go to the ER or... Something is very wrong."

"Dude, you want me to take you?" Duke came closer, but Saman stepped away.

"Nah, I'll be okay. But I should really go."

"Okay, I guess, I'll cover for you, but man, call me and let me know what's going on."

Saman nodded and on a body that felt like a foreign object, shuffled outside and hailed a taxi.

"Take me to the nearest ER. Please."

ENERGY RUSHED up Saman's spine. He'd forgotten about that day with Duke. It was the first sign of his failing kidney. So much had happened since. Cool tears dripped down his cheeks into his hairline. Ever since that trip to the ER he'd felt so much fear and experienced so many hospital visits, so many times he'd thought he would die, and none of it had been his fault. He remembered how happy and hopeful he'd been in San Francisco. *The world was my oyster then*, he thought, *but everything changed. Will I ever feel so carefree again?*

He wiped the tears from his eyes and sucked in a deep breath. The air swirled with new textures and streaks of light. Every touch to his skin was amplified. Feeling a little nauseous again, he drank more water. Thelma was still on her mat, with blankets pulled over her body. Saman was tripping hard now and the grass liquified. The fire vibrated like ripped, red cloth and the ceremony participants blended into flickering shadows.

As he swallowed the cold water, his nausea only increased. Covering his mouth with one hand, Saman staggered toward the trees. *Please don't puke,* he thought. He leaned over at the edge of the clearing and took deep breaths. A dog barked in the distance. Saman peered into the woods. He heard the sound again.

A headlamp hung around his neck and he tried to turn it on, but none of the buttons worked. The sound came again, a dog barking, and rustling leaves. *Did Bāne have a dog? Had someone brought a dog to the ceremony? Or was his mind playing tricks on him?*

Peering into the dark trees, he stepped into the woods. The moon shed enough light to illuminate a footpath cut into the dense foliage. The sound came again, it was definitely a dog whimpering. *Maybe it's stuck, or injured?* Saman thought. To his right, another man was puking behind the bathrooms. Saman inched away from that sound, the sight of the man was making him even sicker.

Behind him, a few women waited by the woods in a line for the porta potty. One lady was staring at him. *Had she heard the dog too?* His stomach heaved. *I thought we weren't supposed to throw up...* he scowled. The other man kept retching into the grass. Saman took a few steps inside the forest; everything quaked and luminous beings leapt out of the shadows and flew away like bats. *They're ghosts*, he thought. *I'm surrounded by ghosts.* The flurry of hallucinations added to his rapidly intensifying motion sickness.

Saman followed the path a few feet deeper into the woods but, distracted by his own visions and not looking down, he stubbed his foot on a large rock and toppled over it before catching himself. Instead of standing, he puked into a pile of leaves. Not much liquid came out of his mouth, but he felt better. In the moonlight, his vomit formed an entire galaxy. He laughed. It was comical, staring at his own puke like it was a wormhole. *I've got to tell Thelma about this,* he thought. *Teleportation by barf.*

As he chuckled, the ghost-beings surrounded him. One was connected to another by a string of light, like a glowing umbilical cord. He traced the string around him in an infinite loop, then stepped forward to try to touch the cords of energy. *Man, I'm tripping hard.* He laughed again. *This is the best trip I've ever had. God bless these crazy chocolates.*

The beings and their strings of light, like pearls thread on a silver chain, formed a circuit between him and a tree trunk. He touched the tree's bark. Beams of light connected him to another tree, and then to another. He moved through the woods. The dog barked again in the distance and then he heard music, faint, almost like a violin playing. How could that be? *Was he hearing the music from under the maloca in the clearing?* But it sounded like it was coming from inside the woods. *Maybe a neighbor is having a party*, he thought. The moon bathed his path in glowing, silver light. Saman reached a banyan tree the width of ten men with roots connecting like thick cables to the earth. As he touched it, energy flowed, a horizontal, blood-pumping artery. The life force, like the forest's heart, beat a rhythm on his palm. He closed his eyes and pulsed with the tree.

AS IF WAKING FROM A DREAM, or was it a memory, Thelma rose, filled with energy from the psilohuasca. Bāne loomed in the fire's flames, watching her. She removed her eye patch and let the heat stroke her injury. An older woman with short, gray hair crossed between them on all fours, knees and palms pressed into the dirt, arching and dipping her spine in the motion of a cat-cow yoga pose. The woman's face contorted to a cartoon swine-face. Swallowing a swirling hive of fibers, blood and tissue, the pig-lady ate from the dirt, which sank into the woman's throat and traveled to her stomach. As if inside an ultra-sound, a fetus with translucent orange skin and blue veins floated within the woman's uterus.

"Hey," Thelma called to the woman, then covered her hand with her mouth, remembering that she wasn't supposed to speak. *I must be seeing things.* But the woman and the baby looked so real. It was a boy child with dark hair. The grass around the woman breathed and steamed. Thelma's heart pounded with fear for the woman, though she didn't understand why.

Something is wrong. I've got to help her.

The woman blinked guinea pig eyes. She resembled a *capybara*, with hair-covered rodent legs and webbed feet. *They have those at zoos*, Thelma thought. She wanted to scream for the woman to stop eating the dirt, that it would hurt the baby, but before she could speak, the child turned into a ball of fibers, then, twisted around, angry, like a dust storm and the old woman spewed out a torrent of brown particles and sinew.

Thelma gasped and her hands flew to her mouth in shock. The woman collapsed and curled into a fetal position. One of the muses rushed to the woman's side and rubbed her shoulder.

Thelma stepped forward, she wanted to help, but Bāne, from the other side of the fire waved his hand at her, as if he knew her thoughts. Like a swatted-fly, Thelma plopped on her mat. She grabbed Saman's arm to tell him what she'd seen, but Saman wasn't there. *He must have gone to the bathroom,* Thelma thought. Dizzy and confused, she tried to process what she'd witnessed. *That poor woman. She's very sick, but she's doing the wrong things to help herself. I must remember this.* Exhausted by the experience and her own emotional reaction, Thelma snuggled into her blanket and drifted into a field of planetary flowers.

When she opened her eyes again, Bāne sat on the grass in front of her, Indian style. Reaching out his thick arms, he touched her shoulders. In the reflection of his brown eyes, this time she felt safe. He was doing something to her on purpose, but it was something good, for her own benefit. Energy from his arms radiated down her body and she placed her palms on his biceps. The connection between them was overwhelming. Thelma's mind emptied and she floated, held by an infinite expansion within the sensation of her own consciousness. Their arms braided together like a rope bridge. Orange, pink and red light bathed the clearing. In a time-lapse, Bāne was an unblinking statue. Then the moment accelerated and passed. Bāne left her alone.

Thelma felt immense and powerful. *I can't forget this feeling*, she thought. *I've got to try that position again with Saman. Saman...* she'd forgotten about him. *Where was he?*

The musicians played faster, more tribal music now, with heavy drums. They chanted and some guests danced in a ring. A woman with thick black hair and a flower-covered dress sang Hawaiian songs in a strong, alto register.

Saman must be around here somewhere, Thelma thought. Under the spell of the music, breathing in and out, sliding into the apex of her journey, another memory took her, picked from a vine, a leaf, another moment in time. She was with her mother and father swimming in the ocean. She remembered the lovely beach house they'd rented, how tan her skin was that year. How sweet the salt-water taffy had tasted. She could feel the heat of the East coast summer sun in her memory. She basked in its bliss.

16

I n the forest, Saman clenched his jaw and focused on the moon. *Had the first mushroom chocolate peaked and worn off?* He suddenly felt more lucid, but his foot hurt, and his gut contracted like a woman in labor. Pain shot from his ankle to his lower leg. The woods swayed, a dark green lung, expanding and collapsing.

Did I twist my ankle or something? Dizzy, he leaned against a tree and tried to examine his foot, but lost his balance and almost fell face-first.

"Hello," he said, suddenly worried he was lost. "Can anyone hear me?"

No answer.

Don't panic.

I should go back to the clearing, he thought, but didn't move. Slowing his breath, to distract from the pain in his ankle, he tried to think about something pleasant. *What was there to think about? What would make me happy to imagine?*

But it wasn't his choice to decide.

THE HAWAIIAN GRASS shimmered in the moonlight. Shapes of people littered the ground, like miniature marooned whales. Thelma rubbed her eyes. Saman's blankets were crumpled on his mat. She wanted to sleep, but *where was Saman? Had he gone under the maloca?* She got up to look for him. Stepping around people on the ground, she started to get nervous. *Where had Saman gone?*

Thelma worked her way around the circle again, but he wasn't there. She went to the bathrooms; one stall was empty. A woman came out of the other stall. No Saman. Anxiety clutched at Thelma. *Something is wrong. Saman should be here.* Bāne had instructed everyone to stay in the clearing until he blew the final conch horn. *Had Saman gone back to the main house?*

Maybe I missed him in the dark, she thought. Everyone was zoned out and her own brain felt foggy and strange.

Returning to their mats, she fished around inside Saman's bookbag to see if there was a flashlight, but there wasn't. Still on the mushrooms, she struggled to zip Saman's bag. *What if he had a panic attack? What if he was sick? What if, what if, what if. Calm the fuck down,* she thought. *Even if he went back to the house, I'm sure he's fine.* But she wasn't sure.

Her breath came in shallow gasps and she circled the perimeter of the clearing. She'd convinced Saman to do the ceremony and now he was missing. *Wasn't it her responsibility to find him?* Moving stiff, like a robot, she found the trail back to the house. *Should I go back?* But staring at the forest, it was so dark. She couldn't see more than an arm's length ahead.

Saman, she whispered into the woods.

No answer.

Her muscles tensed. Bāne had said not to leave the clearing, but Saman had left, clearly. He was nowhere else.

Taking a step forward, a twig snapped under her foot. She stopped. *This is stupid. I at least need a flashlight.*

Turning back, she went to find Bāne. Maybe he had a flashlight. Thelma found him under the maloca, seated with his eyes closed. A small circle of guests meditated around him. Lingering at the edge of the structure's wooden platform, she hesitated. If she disturbed Bāne now, she'd be breaking the rules of the ceremony.

A hand touched her shoulder. Thelma spun around, hoping it was Saman, but it was Dan. She grabbed his arm, and he registered surprise on his face, but let her guide him away from the circle.

"I'm sorry to bother you," she whispered, "but I can't find Saman."

Dan put one finger to his lip to shush her, then shrugged and opened his palms to say, 'I don't know.'

"He's not here. Have you seen him?" she whispered.

Dan shook his head 'no.' He pointed to his watch and mouthed, "It's almost over."

She tried to look at Dan's watch, but the numbers were blurry because she was still tripping. Frustration brewed in her chest, "I need to find Saman," she said in a louder whisper.

Dan leaned closer, "I'm sure he's around."

"No, he's missing," her voice quivered. "Do you have a flashlight?"

Dan shook his head 'no'.

She pursed her lips and scowled. Dan wasn't understanding the gravity of her situation; she'd have to interrupt Bāne.

WHEN SAMAN WOKE, he was next to Thelma's warm body. He pulled her closer, burying his face in her honey-colored hair, his arms on her flat, soft stomach.

She rolled to face him and kissed his cheek. "Are you nervous?"

"Yes. I can't stop my mind from racing."

She hugged him to her chest, "That's normal babe, but you'll do great."

How can she be so calm? he wondered.

Before he could respond, pain yanked him away. *No, no, no*, he thought. *Not again. Please God, not again.*

Thelma had been a figment of the psilohuasca. This was not his bed. *Where am I?*

He was delirious and fucked-up.

I need help.

Did Bāne blow the conch shell? Or am I only hearing things?

Saman shifted his legs on Hawaii's cool earth. His stomach flooded with pain and his chest tightened with fear. *I need to go back,* he thought. Hoisting himself up with all the strength in his arms, he limped a few feet, then the pain and bodily sensations overwhelmed him.

"Fuck!" Saman screamed. He sank into a cluster of ferns.

The psilohuasca was not finished. His trip was incomplete.

He rolled on his back. Stars shone through the tree branches and the moon, an orb of light, floated in the night; in its luminance, a spider web glistened. The insect moved in circles over its strings with legs like pine needles. *Does it see me? Do spiders see in the dark?*

Saman felt terrible, but he was also in rapture of the large insect. He stretched out on the forest floor and lost all sense of time and place. Shadows snaked across the leaves around him and patterns of green, blue, red and orange colors moved in rotation like endless panels of stained glassed windows. Each glowed and multiplied, then became a million oil lamps, then candles, then the face of his father, but Saman snapped open his eyes. He didn't want to see his dead dad, not right now.

"You're fine," he said out loud, speaking to the spider. "Everything's fine."

He shut his eyes again. His father was gone, replaced with the eyes of the spider and its long legs spinning complex geometric designs, drawings on the black paper of night. Pain spread to his chest and he rubbed the skin over his heart. The motion sent particles like broken glass shattering through his bloodstream. The world reverberated, rippling around him, like it might explode. It was too much to look at, or to feel, so he shrank inside himself, but behind his eye lids, he saw the face of a girl he wanted to forget. He recognized her blond hair and black-lined eyes, her glare of contempt.

No, he thought. *Not her*, but it was too late.

It was Kayla, his prior intern.

The spider's web twinkled in the starlight. *Why her? Why Kayla?* Saman asked himself, eyes open again.

Because you lied to her and you lied about her. A voice answered, *You lied to yourself too.*

And Saman knew it was true. There'd been so many lies, white lies, to avoid showing her things, to pretend like he had everything under control, to keep her from succeeding in his job.

Why did I do that?

Because you're afraid and full of shame, the voice replied, *because you want to keep yourself behind a locked door, like you're a dark secret. Who else have you lied to?*

Saman shook his head. Thelma, Reed, his mother, his

sister, his boss Ron; he'd lied to so many people. He'd concealed how he was struggling, just as he'd done with his old coworker, Duke, when he first got sick, downplaying his symptoms. *But why?*

Because you're always afraid, the voice said. *You're afraid that you'll lose the things and people you love, the work you love. You're afraid that you'll lose everything, because you've already lost a lot. You've lost more than most, but it's okay; we all eventually lose everything. But when you lie, you lose yourself, and no one wants a lost man. Stop hiding, stop lying, and be true.*

Saman nodded.

I want to be true.

In dirt-covered hands, he buried his face and sobbed, ugly gut-wrenching cries that vibrated his core and echoed through the woods.

BEFORE THELMA COULD APPROACH BĀNE, Dan put his hand on her upper arm to stop her. "Hold on," he said, "let's calm down for a second. When was the last time you saw your husband?"

She shook her head, "I don't know," she whispered, "Close to the start of the ceremony maybe? I'm worried."

"Let's check the bathrooms first," Dan offered.

"Please," Thelma said, "I've already done that. I want to check the trail; I just need a flashlight."

"Listen, stay here and I'll tell River what's going on. You can't go by yourself," Dan said. "You can fall. It's not safe."

"Well, if it's not safe for me, then what about for Saman?" she pressed, speaking louder.

Dan hesitated, and before he could respond, Bāne loomed behind him, no doubt drawn by the noise of their tense exchange. "What's going on?" Bāne asked in a deep, but quiet voice.

"My husband, Saman, I think he's gone into the woods or left the clearing. I can't find him and I'm worried," Thelma gushed.

Bāne frowned. A few other guests gathered behind him to listen, concerned.

Bāne raised his arms into the air, palms facing out, "Everyone, please relax and return to your mats. A guest wandered out of the clearing. This happens sometimes. There's no cause for alarm."

"I can help. I've got a flashlight," a man offered.

Dan gestured to the man with the flashlight. "Hey, yeah, I'll go with Bernie and check the main house, see if he's there."

A woman also spoke, "Does your husband have long, black curly hair?

Thelma nodded, "Yes, did you see him?"

"We were both by the bathrooms, then he went into the woods. I figured he was going to pee, but, thinking about it, I didn't see him come back."

Bāne motioned towards the portable toilet stalls, "Okay, let's go check the woods behind the bathrooms. Thelma, wait here for us."

"I'll come with you," Thelma said.

"Please stay here in case he comes back."

She raked her fingers through her blond hair, "I'd prefer to look for him."

"No. Dan and Bernie have more experience with this type of search."

Dan patted her shoulder, "It'll be okay. We'll find him."

As the three men left to search for Saman, Thelma followed them with her eyes to the edge of the clearing by the bathrooms. The white beams of their flashlights caught on leaves, bouncing in the dark, then faded into the forest. Frustrated about being left behind, and still tripping more than she wanted to be, she paced in front of the bathroom stalls. *Where was Saman and why had he left in the first place?*

One of the muses came to Thelma's side. "I'm River," she said. "I'm sure your husband will be fine. He probably wanted to be alone."

Thelma shook her head, "Something's wrong; he's lost, or maybe sick, or hurt. I can feel it in my gut."

River held Thelma's gaze for a second then nodded with a knowing expression. "I see. I can understand your concern," the muse said. "Bāne will find him. He could have only gone so far. Let's wait by the fire."

Thelma shook her head, "No thank you. I prefer to wait here."

"Okay, I'll wait with you," the muse said, then stayed beside Thelma like a watchdog.

17

S aman lay under the stars and thought about what it would feel like to finally die.

Maybe I'll die tonight, he thought. *That's what the universe wants from me anyway.*

The weight of the psilohuasca pressed him to the ground. The spider above him rested like a charm on a silver necklace. Tension seized his torso. He was in so much *pain*.

Pain. The word traveled to his brain. He imagined it traveling through his neurons like a drop of dew on the spider's web. The web was like the constellations and he sensed the scale of the universe inside his cells.

Through the forest, he heard the sound of the conch shell — one, two, three times.

Panic flooded his body. How could he still be tripping so hard when the ceremony was almost over? *Did the opioids in my system mess with the psilohuasca?*

His heart pounded. *I need to get up,* he thought, but he couldn't move. It was like the weight of gravity itself had increased.

Then he heard the beep of a machine.

In an instant, he was back on the operating table below bright fluorescent tube lights and surrounded by hospital staff. The room smelled of chemicals and blood. He screamed. This time he could scream. The staff turned and acknowledged him. They had insect faces. *I've been split in two*, he realized. One of him was unconscious on the table, eyes rolled back in his head like a dead animal, and one of him was at the door, as if he was ready to leave.

"Stop!" the one of him by the door screamed, "You're hurting me!"

The surgeon shrugged, "But we've got to finish. We can't leave you cut open."

Saman shook his head, "You've got to help me. I'm going to wake up."

"We're sorry," the doctor replied from behind his face shield and surgical mask.

"His heartbeat is really erratic," a nurse said.

On the table, the hole in Saman's side gaped and bled like they'd pulled out a rib.

"Don't let me die!" he yelled from the doorway.

The heart monitor beeped faster, then flatlined.

The hospital vanished. He was under the tree, under the atmosphere, under the moon, under the stars, under the solar system, under the galaxy, and so on, and so on, for as far as light could travel.

"Hello," he shouted. "Can anyone hear me?"

No answer.

"Help, I'm lost!"

Leaves crunched in the distance.

"Help!" Saman shouted again, using all his strength. "I'm injured."

"Saman!" A man's voice in the distance.

"Yes, I'm here. I'm here."

"We're coming!"

Pain held Saman's chest tight like a tourniquet. The forest gave way, branches broke, and footsteps thudded on the earth. "I'm here," Saman pushed out the words again, as if speaking with a stick of butter lodged between his lips.

A man emerged from the shadows and shined a flashlight on Saman's face. Bāne and Dan appeared beside him.

"Are you okay?" Dan pulled Saman off the ground.

"Ouch!" Saman shrieked as his ankle buckled under his body weight.

"Oh sorry, mate, what happened?"

Saman leaned into Dan, "I came to throw up, but got turned around and hurt my foot."

The Hawaiian man dropped to his knees and pointed the flashlight at Saman's leg. "It's hard to see anything," the man said.

"We should take him to the house," Dan suggested.

"I don't know how much weight I can put on my foot, but I'll do my best." Saman winced.

Bāne gave Dan a nod, "Let's get him out of here."

Dan slid under Saman's right arm, and Bāne went under the other. They lugged Saman through the woods.

"I'm so sorry," Saman said. He wanted to say more, but pain consumed him.

As they reached the tree line, Thelma rushed to Saman.

"Oh, my God, are you okay?"

"I'm sorry. I hurt my leg," he breathed.

They lay Saman onto a blanket by the fire.

"What happened?" Thelma knelt beside him. "Babe, I'm so glad you're okay. I was so worried."

Saman drank water from a thermos one of the Muses

offered him. His thoughts were muddy. "I did something to my foot." Tears threatened to storm in his eyes.

"This is River. She's a nurse," Bāne said.

Thelma moved to the side, and River examined his leg.

"Thelma," Saman said, tugging on her shirt, "I saw the spider. I saw your spider." He was so happy to see her.

"What? What spider? Did it bite you?"

"No, it was making a web, a beautiful web."

"It might be an insect bite," River said," It's hard to tell."

"Are there poisonous spiders here?" Thelma asked.

River scrutinized Saman's leg with the flashlight.

"No, it didn't bite me," Saman said. He squeezed Thelma's hand "I told you, it was weaving a web."

"Y'all take him back to the house," Bāne said to Dan and River. "I gotta close the ceremony."

Dan nodded. "Of course. Let's get you cleaned up."

"I don't know if I can walk."

"Are there poisonous spiders out here?" Thelma repeated her question.

"Do you have any other symptoms besides pain in your foot?" River asked, still ignoring Thelma.

He nodded, "Yes. I might puke again."

River said something, but Saman had stopped listening. A cold sweat covered him; he shivered.

"No," Thelma said. "You look awful. We're going back."

Did she read my mind? he wondered.

"Let's go," Dan said. He pulled Saman up, and they headed out of the clearing.

As they descended the hill, the black earth shifted under Saman's feet. *The psilohuasca.* He remembered watching a movie as a kid where a bear ate mushrooms and then the filmmakers used technicolor distortion to convey that the mushrooms poisoned the bear. *I'm like that bear right now; only I poisoned myself*. Shadows and green flecks of light snaked in the corners of his vision. He limped on one leg, leaning on Dan. With every step, it grew harder to breathe.

They reached the main house, and he collapsed on a sofa. River rushed to the kitchen and returned with a cooking pot full of ice and a washcloth. She elevated his leg.

He stared at the ceiling. Every muscle ached.

"You'll be fine," River said, "But you need to see a doctor in case it's a spider bite."

"I just need to sleep." Saman exhaled. He wanted to lay in bed with Thelma in their room, alone.

Thelma grabbed River by the shoulders and spun her around, "Are there poisonous spiders here?"

River hesitated.

"Answer me," Thelma said with panic in her voice. "Are there poisonous spiders?"

"Yes, there are poisonous spiders on the island, but let's not rush to conclusions. We don't know if anything even bit him."

"It's fine," Saman said, "but I need some pain medication. I probably twisted my ankle. I have some in my bag. Thelma, can you get it for me?"

"You can't take those pills," Thelma said, "Not with the psilohuasca already in your system. And your ankle is red like something bit you."

"What pills?" River asked, frowning.

"He has like prescription painkillers leftover from a surgery."

River's eyes widened. "Were they on the approved medication list? When did you last take them? Everyone was warned not to take any unapproved medication before the ceremony."

"Thelma didn't know I was taking them," Saman groaned, "But I didn't take them today, anyway."

River nodded, "Okay, good. When did you last take them and what were they?"

He didn't answer. He didn't want to lie. "I tripped," he said instead, half remembering stumbling into the tree with the spider.

"I'm going to clean you up. Your arm is scratched. Otherwise, you could get a staph infection," River said.

Thelma turned to Dan, "What about your wife? Can she come look at him?"

"She's delivering a baby, remember?"

"Fuck," Thelma said, "Should we call 911?"

"No. Don't call 911," Saman said. "Really, I'm fine."

"Maybe he's just having a bad trip," Dan offered.

"Yes, I am," Saman said. "Thank you for getting me here, but I'll be fine." He winced as he spoke, the discomfort in his stomach increased. He needed to get to a bathroom. "You guys are overreacting."

"Babe, I'm taking you to the hospital," Thelma said, her voice rising an octave.

"No, you aren't. You're overreacting," Saman snapped and teetered forward, "I need to go to bed." A jolt of pain rushed up his leg. He clutched the sofa's arm and his muscles tensed. He wanted to vomit. *No. No. NO.* "I'm not going to the fucking hospital. I told you, I'm fine."

Thelma touched his shoulder. "Honey, calm down."

River turned to Dan, "Are you sober enough to drive?"

Dan shook his head, "Not at all. You have a melty-face. That's where I'm at."

River nodded. "Me too. None of us should drive."

The room spun. Saman's stomach churned. Overwhelmed, he leaned forward and threw up on the floor.

"Saman," Thelma grabbed his shoulder, "that's it. We're going to the hospital."

"No," he slurred, and wiped the vomit from his chin.

"I'll drive him," Thelma said.

"No. I just needed to puke."

"Come on!" Thelma pulled on Saman's arm.

Saman rolled away from her.

Thelma's voice rose, almost frantic, she exclaimed, "I can't let anything else bad happen to you!"

"I'm not going!" The last thing he wanted was to be in a hospital room. *No way.* His body clenched into a ball. Clutching his stomach, he refused to cooperate.

"Saman!" Thelma, in tears, strained to get him off the sofa.

He resisted.

"Look, man, everything is going to be okay, but you've got to help us," Dan said, trying to help Thelma lift Saman.

"I just want to go to bed." Saman rolled over and was sick again. Bile sprayed over the cream tile floor.

"Please, babe," His wife knelt beside him and touched his shoulder, "If anything happens to you, I'll never forgive myself."

"It already happened." He gripped the edge of the sofa, yanked himself to standing, and with all his remaining energy, bolted towards the bedroom.

"Saman, stop!" Thelma called, but he forced himself to run. *I'm not going to the hospital,* he thought, *hell no. No way.* He reached the bedroom and locked the door behind him. He'd ride this out. After all, nothing was worse than the pain he'd already experienced in his life.

"Please, open the door. Saman, come on. Open it!" Thelma cried from the hallway, turning the door handle back and forth and pounding her fists on the wood.

But he wouldn't. He wasn't going to the hospital. "I'm sorry Thelma, I told you. I'm not going."

"Saman, don't do this!" Thelma's voice was strained and angry,

"I love you, but go away!" he shouted, "and don't you dare call 911. If you do, I swear to God, Thelma, I'll file for a divorce. I'm not kidding. I need to do this on my own."

"Open the door!" She rattled the knob and attempted to force her way into the room.

Pressing his weight into the door, he slid to the floor.

Thelma screamed his name.

He leaned into his pain and swallowed it like a spider eating a fly.

RUNNING THROUGH THE HOUSE, Thelma searched for River. *I need the bedroom key; I've got to get Saman out.* The living room was deserted. "River?" she called, "Dan!"

No answer. *Where had they gone? They were just there?* Or was time moving faster than she realized? Suddenly, Thelma felt very confused and disoriented. She wandered out to the patio and sat down on a sofa.

Why wouldn't Saman go to the hospital? A spider bite could be lethal. What if his single kidney couldn't process the spider's venom? What if he'd already collapsed and was unconscious? What if, if, if . . . Her heart pounded like an intruder in her chest. She needed that key.

I'll find Bāne, even if it means running all the way to the clearing. I'll make him give me the key. She got up and bolted past the swimming pool. Clouds obstructed the moon and the stars. *Shit, it's dark.* She still didn't have a flashlight.

Thelma entered the woods, breathing in sharp gasps.

Rocks and roots created hazards even in the daylight; if she wasn't careful, she'd fall. The track forked in two, and she almost smacked into a tree. She panted, not remembering the split. *Am I on the correct path?* It looked steeper than she remembered, but maybe it was because she was tired and going uphill now? Exhausted from the late hour and the psilohuasca, she wanted to stop, but instead she pressed on, hiking deeper into the woods. After what seemed like an hour, she thought, *I must be near the clearing.* But as soon as the words crossed her mind, the trail dead-ended into a thicket.

"Fuck!" she shouted into the forest.

She backtracked, inching sideways to move faster without losing her balance. *I'm lost. How could I let this happen? I must have taken the wrong trail back at the fork.*

"Thelma, is that you? Are you okay?" A woman's voice came from behind her. Bobbing flashlights approached. It was River and the Hawaiian man from the ceremony. "What are you doing out here?"

"I'm fine," Thelma wheezed, "But Saman— he, Saman locked himself in the bedroom. I need to find Bāne and get the key."

River touched her shoulder, "Come with us back to the house."

The Hawaiian man added, "Bāne's closing the ceremony."

"No, I have to get the key," Thelma said. "Please, take me back to the clearing."

"It's not safe for you to be wandering around. Let's get you inside and then we'll check on Saman." River said.

"If you won't take me to the clearing, then I'll go on my own." Thelma trudged away.

"You're headed in the wrong direction," River shouted.

Thelma pivoted and marched back past River and the man, but they grabbed her and dragged her to the main house protesting and crying.

⁂

PAIN SPLINTERED in Saman's body as he crawled across the bedroom floor to his suitcase. In the haze of his distorted vision, he found his bottle of prescription pain pills. Pouring the medication into his hands — five pills remained. The drugs resembled tiny round insects in his palm, the size of lady bugs. *I could take one or two,* Saman thought. The pain in his ankle and gut would fade away in thirty minutes. But he remembered the spider in the moonlight, the voice, the truth.

Still holding the pills, he closed his eyes and saw a song like an animation. It reminded him of a documentary about gypsy music. In one scene, an old man in a tattered dress with white hair and hallow cheeks stood in front of a dead tree. He played a mournful refrain on a battered violin. As the man played, Saman realized it was his uncle. Though they'd never met, the man resembled the photos of his uncle. This isn't a scene from a film, Saman thought, this is a message.

As his uncle played the violin, an older woman came from the shadows and stood beside him. She had long white hair and wrinkles around her dark brown eyes. *My uncle's wife*, Saman thought. She sang a bold, fierce melody.

> *I'm alive, a speck on this complex web of*
>   *time.*
> *You can't kill me,*
> *The universe already tried,*

a hundred times,
with needles and knives,
with ideas and lies,
But the truth survives.

His aunt bellowed the lyrics, while his uncle played the violin. Saman lay on the cool wood floor and listened.

She repeated the words, *The truth survives.*

The repeating melody became an affirmation, a rope to grip and hold. It pulled him out of his misery. The strength of the song stemmed and grew, twisting the chords into a physical cord that he climbed like a beanstalk.

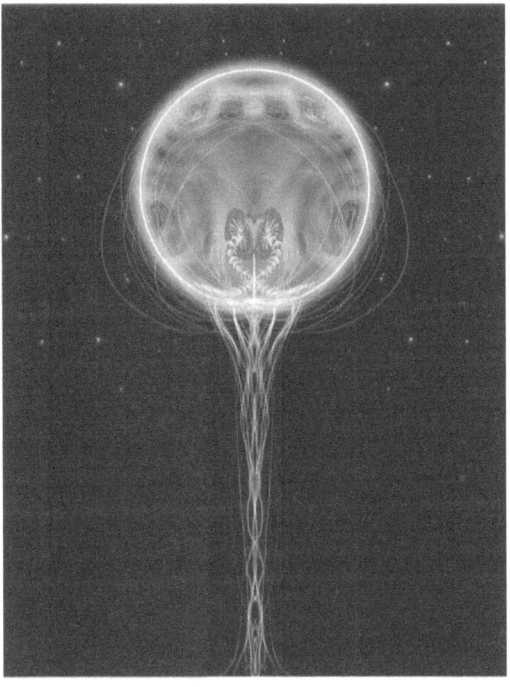

Light filled the psilohuasca's vision and his family faded

into a white abyss. Then there were words, not written or spoken, but sensed.

> *My love, she's winding down.*
> *My love of life, it's underground.*
> *Let me experience this bliss,*
> *this fading oyster's dream*
> *the pearl that I am.*

It was the song he'd heard during his kidney transplant. Saman opened his eyes and cried; his tears flowed out with each soaring note. As he released his sadness, a new image came to him; in the white space, a spider's silver web surfaced and formed a sac. It enveloped him and from within the web was his kidney, the surgery, the bad dreams, everything. Inside the silken container, Thelma pointed her camera at him and took a picture. *I will tell her the truth,* he thought. *She deserves the best of me. I will support her the way she supported me.* The power of his imagination, paired with the psilohuasca, drew him deeper into Thelma's camera's lens, like a prism; he passed through its glass. In tomorrow's future, he would live in truth and correct the lies he'd told.

Saman pulled himself from the web and reentered the reality of Bāne's bedroom. He crawled to the adjoining bathroom. The site of the toilet made his stomach heave, and he lunged forward, throwing up into the porcelain bowl. As he flushed the toilet, he sprinkled the remaining pain pills like ashes into the swirling bile. *Goodbye, pain,* he said to himself, and collapsed onto the tile floor. His suffering was still there, but it didn't matter. He would see Thelma in the morning and tell her everything. He would describe the spider, his uncle, and the song. It was all connected.

Wanting to get in bed, Saman gathered his strength,

then pulled himself from the ground and slid out of his dirty clothes. His foot still hurt, but he ignored it. Naked, he gazed at the moon through the bedroom window. Outside, all was quiet.

I'll be okay, he thought. *I don't have to hide or be afraid or ashamed. Each note plays, then floats away. Every song is a state of change.*

> *Let me experience this bliss, this fading*
> *oyster's dream*
> *the pearl that I am.*

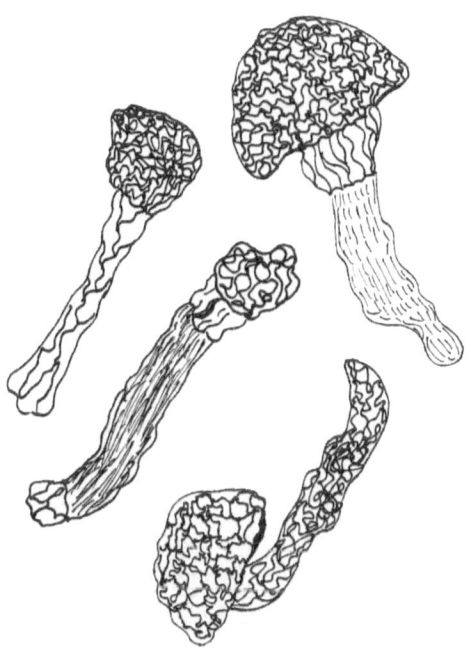

18

Strangers lounged on patio chairs outside on the terrace, laughing and chatting. Sunlight cracked into Thelma's vision like a hammer on glass. She almost rubbed her face, then remembered her eye patch. She was prone on a plush sofa. *Oh, my God, how long have I been asleep?* The night returned to her in splintered pieces — Saman locking the door, her lost in the woods, River and another man dragging her to the house. *No. It couldn't be. How had she let herself fall asleep without checking on Saman?* Her head was stuffed with disbelief. *Was Saman okay? What time was it?* Her memory wasn't a dream. She needed to find Saman.

Sweaty, she hurried to their bedroom and turned the doorknob; it opened. *Thank God.* But her heart sank. The room was empty. *Where had Saman gone? Had someone taken him to the hospital?*

In the hallway, a man's voice called her. "Thelma!" It was Bāne, shirtless, wearing a piece of floral Hawaiian fabric wrapped around his thick, muscular abdomen like a skirt.

"Have you seen Saman?" Thelma blurted.

"Yep. Saman's fine." Bāne put his hands on his hips and squinted at her, "Are *you* fine?"

"I need to find Saman."

"He's in the kitchen." Bāne cocked his head to the side. "You had quite a night, *Florida Woman*."

"He's okay?" She stumbled on her words, "I, I'm . . ." before she could finish her sentence, Bāne embraced her, wrapping his thick arms around her body. He pulled her to his firm torso and held her like a parent comforting a child.

She stiffened, wanting to pull away. There was no time for hugs, she needed to find Saman.

"I . . . I'm so sorry," she responded, the words muffled against Bāne's bare skin. "I didn't mean to disrupt the . . ."

"Shhhh," Bāne interrupted her. "We had quite a moment together last night. Do you remember?"

A moment? Thelma blinked. *What?* Her mind was fuzzy. "I... I'm sorry, I don't know. I'm sorry, but I need to find my husband. He isn't in our room."

Bāne chuckled, "Your husband already apologized, and I've accepted his apology."

What? What had Saman told him?

"Now, tell me — why are you apologizing?" With one hand, he lifted her chin, and they locked eyes.

His words disarmed her. "I . . . I don't know."

"Yes, you do."

Blood rushed to her cheeks. She had to leave. *What did he want her to say? Why was he asking her this?* "Um, I don't remember exactly what happened. I thought the ceremony would help my husband, but... but he was missing last night. I was looking for him because I was worried."

"And did it help him?"

"It . . . You'll have to ask him." *This conversation needs to end*, Thelma thought.

Bāne grinned and chuckled again. He let go of her chin. "You're right. Let's go find him, and then I want you to speak to the group."

Her heart flapped like a fish in a net as she followed Bāne. *What was he talking about? Speak to the group?* She just needed to find Saman. As soon as they walked into the kitchen, she spotted her husband sitting on a stool by a marble kitchen island, wearing clean clothes, and surrounded by Roberta, Dan, and River.

"Saman," Thelma wanted to collapse with relief. She ran to him and threw her arms around his neck. "Why didn't you wake me? I'm so glad you're okay."

"Hey, my love," Saman said, as if nothing had happened. He kissed her on the lips, then hugged her to his chest. "I'm fine now. Roberta came this morning and examined me. She took care of my ankle," he pointed to his leg, propped on the island's ledge and wrapped in a brace. "I didn't want to disturb you, you looked so peaceful on the sofa."

Thelma squeezed him, "I'm so sorry that I made you come. I shouldn't have forced you."

"Shh, it's okay. You were right. It was good for me," Saman pulled a leaf out of her hair. "I'm sorry I was so diffi-cult last night."

Her tears of relief dampened his t-shirt. "I was so worried," she whispered.

"I also have something to tell you," Saman said.

"What?" She stepped back.

"I'm so sorry I didn't tell you sooner."

"Tell me what?"

Saman reached for Thelma's hand and held it with both of his. She tensed up, uncomfortable that River, Roberta, Dan, and Bāne were watching their personal exchange.

"I believed I was fine. I pretended I was fine, but I lied.

I'm not fine. I need help, and one thing I need help with is getting off those pain killers."

"What?" This was not what she had expected him to tell her. She'd thought he was going to admit he needed to go back to therapy.

"Yes. I've been buying painkillers from Reed. I'm so sorry. I've thrown the rest away, and when we're done with the closing ceremony, Roberta will take me to her clinic, and help me make a recovery plan."

Thelma's breath caught in her chest. Suddenly, everything made sense — his mood swings, the way he always looked tired, his nightmares. A girlfriend from university had been addicted to pain pills, and Thelma remembered that the drugs had caused her friend to have terrible dreams.

"I should have told you, but I was in denial. I also dropped out of school before it even started. I withdrew my application, but I do want to go back, I was just afraid of failing or dragging us into some kind of financial ruin. I was afraid to let you down."

Thelma didn't know what to say.

"I love you." He hugged her again.

"I love you, too." She buried her face in his hair and inhaled his scent, allowing herself to sink into his embrace.

"Well, I hate to rush this lovely reunion," Bāne cleared his throat, "but we should make our way outside. Saman is in skilled hands with Roberta."

"Yes," Roberta said, "We're going to get him through this. He's lucky he isn't having worse withdrawal symptoms. It won't be easy, but it could be much worse. Thankfully, his addiction was in an early stage, from what he's told me."

Thelma looked around, embarrassed. This was too much to process. "Sorry and thank you."

"No reason to apologize," Dan grinned, "Some crazy shit always happens at these ceremonies."

"I thought a spider had bitten Saman and I panicked." Thelma admitted.

"I didn't find any bite," Roberta said.

"Spiders are rare here," Bāne added.

"He sprained his ankle, but not too badly. Just try not to walk too much," Roberta offered.

Thelma nodded, overwhelmed. Saman's hidden drug addiction sunk in. *How was I so disconnected that I didn't realize he had a problem?* she wondered.

"The important thing is what you've gained from the ceremony, and what the others learned from dealing with their reactions to your discomfort," Bāne said.

Saman nodded, "I gained a lot. Thank you, truly. It was life-changing."

Bāne winked, "That's why we're here."

"Yes, I had so many revelations." Saman squeezed Thelma's hand.

"You can share them with the group," Bāne said. "Let's return to the terrace for integration."

"My favorite part," River said.

Bāne wrapped his biceps around River's slight frame and kissed her cheek. "Let's go, my muse."

River beamed.

Thelma shook her head. "I need a minute."

"See you guys outside," Dan said, and the group left them alone in the kitchen.

"Everything will be fine." Saman kissed Thelma on the lips, "and I'll accept the settlement. We won't go to court and I'll give half the money to you, for everything you've had to put up with."

"I can't believe you were taking those pills this whole

time, and I didn't realize it." Thelma blinked back tears, "I'm so sorry I wasn't there for you."

"Don't be." He took her hands, "How could you have known? I was dishonest, and you didn't deserve that. I won't do it again. I never want to hide anything from you."

They held each other for a few minutes longer, then Saman led her to the swimming pool where the rest of the participants waited. They found a spot on a love seat. Another muse in a white dress struck a gold and black gong with a wood mallet. The sound reverberated through the estate.

Bāne raised his arms to the sun, then brought them to a prayer position at his heart and addressed the crowd. "Before we break into our integration circles, Thelma will share her experience. She is a gifted seer of truths." He gestured to Thelma.

Thelma's body tightened. *Why her?*

"And don't leave out any details." Bāne beckoned for her to step forward.

Heart thumping, she made her way to the front of the pool, trying not to tremble.

Bāne passed her a microphone. As if in a bad dream, Thelma tried to hold it steady with shaking hands. *What should I say? What did I see?* She forced herself to remember. *The guinea pig woman.* Thelma took a deep breath, "I saw many things last night, but one of my most powerful visions was about you." She pointed to the gray-haired lady and described the woman, the animal shape, the baby, and the tornado of dirt.

When she finished, Bāne called the gray-haired woman forward. "Does Thelma's vision resonate with you?"

The woman wiped her wet eyes. "Yes. It does. I, I haven't told many people this, and I'm embarrassed to say it, but I've struggled with bulimia for many years, and what she described makes me think of that."

"I'm so sorry," Thelma said and instinctively went and hugged the woman.

"Secrets are deadly," Bāne said. "You must release them, or they will cause inner rot." He turned to the group, "Has anyone else experienced bulimia or know someone who has?"

A younger woman raised her hand and spoke, "My older sister had bulimia. She went to a treatment program for it and recovered."

Bāne motioned to the lady from Thelma's vision, "Connect with your new friend and her sister about this and we also have a doctor here who can help."

Roberta waived to the woman.

"Thank you." The older lady bowed her head, and sat beside the younger girl, who hugged her.

"Now, let's break into groups for further integration," Bāne said, then divided them into new circles.

Each person described their experience and takeaways from the ceremony. Thelma wanted to sit beside Saman, but Bāne had separated them. When the integration was over, everyone gravitated to a buffet of fruit, bread, eggs, and juice. Thelma found Saman sitting on the ground with Bāne and the three muses. River sat to Bāne's left, and another muse lay across his lap.

"Sit with us," Bāne said as she approached. "Saman was telling the story about how you foresaw your former lover's death." He laughed, "Ya know, some light brunch conversation."

Thelma grimaced; her ex's passing was still painful to remember.

Bāne continued, "Maria told me you were gifted, and I can see what she meant."

Thelma hesitated, then sat beside Saman.

"Ladies, can you give me a moment alone with Thelma and Saman?" Bāne asked.

The muses nodded, and in unison, wandered off.

"Do they live here?" Saman asked.

"Sometimes. When they want." Bāne's eyes twinkled.

"Cool," Saman responded.

"Yes, it is," Bāne said.

Thelma shifted her legs, trying to find a comfortable position on the grass. *Was Bāne going to lecture them?* She wanted to go back to bed. *Why bother even talking about this when they were leaving so soon?*

Bāne leaned forward, "Saman and I have something important to discuss with you."

Thelma looked at the two men, "You do?"

"Yes honey, I'd like to offer you and Saman a job here on the island."

Thelma arched her eyebrows. "Really?"

Saman nodded. "And I've agreed." He grinned. "I mean, if you agree, too."

"What?" Thelma's jaw shot forward and her eyes widened. "I don't understand."

"Bāne has a job for us," Saman said, turning to face her, "and I want to take it."

She was so confused. *A job?* "What kind of job?" she stammered, "We're going home tomorrow."

"Nonsense," Bāne said and laughed. "Saman needs to go to Roberta's clinic, or I'll never hear the end of it, and I value Dan's friendship very much. I don't want to cause trouble with Dan's old lady." He laughed at his own joke, shaking the muscles ridged along his abdomen.

"Plus, you need to go to the eye doctor," Saman said.

"I can go in Florida," Thelma couldn't believe they were having this discussion.

"Hear Bāne out," Saman rubbed her shoulder.

"Yes," Bāne grinned. "I've been looking for someone like you two. I want to expand the reach of these retreats and produce videos, start a podcast, and create marketing materials, do more photos. I need people who understand the medicine and have production skills. Saman said he does audio and you do photos and videos. That's exactly what I need — a perfect fit. Plus, Sunita is leaving to do a PhD on the mainland, so I could also use a ceremony assistant with your visionary skills."

"I'm flattered, but I really don't have much experience with video. I'm more of a photographer," Thelma squinted at Saman, her jaw agape.

"Your videos are great," Saman chimed in, "Don't undersell yourself. I showed Bāne some of your social media."

Thelma swatted a mosquito off her thigh. *How could they stay? What about their house? Saman's cat? Her photography clients? This was too much.*

Saman squeezed her hand, "Bāne said Hilo has an amazing ecoacoustics program. I'll study part time, and you'll be taking photos. We can both do what we love."

Her mind swirled. *When had Bāne and Saman cooked up this plan?* "What about StanGetz?" she asked.

"We'll bring StanGetz here. He'll love Hawaii." Excitement danced in Saman's eyes.

"Who is StanGetz?" Bāne asked.

"My cat," Saman replied.

Bāne laughed, "Cats are welcome, they have to quarantine, but don't worry, I know people at the airport who can help." Bāne stretched his well-defined legs, sticking them out of the fabric of his skirt. "I also have a vacation rental that needs minor repairs, but you can live there, and I'll pay you both a salary."

Saman gazed at Thelma with the most joy she'd seen since their wedding day. "This feels right, my love."

"Your mother will flip out."

Saman shrugged, "What's new?"

"I don't know, it's..." she trailed off. The two men waited on her response. *What would staying really mean?* She was too tired to consider all the details. She'd say yes now, then sleep and reevaluate her answer tomorrow. She slowly nodded. "Okay, babe."

"Great!" Bāne clapped his hands together, "Amazing. I'm so excited. Y'all will love it here."

"Thank you, my love." Saman rubbed her shoulder.

"May I ask what other kind of work you do?" Thelma inquired, realizing that Saman was accepting an offer from a man they knew very little about. No way the lavish estate came from money earned by hosting hippie mushroom ceremonies. "I feel like I know you from somewhere, like from TV?"

His face lit up, "Have you heard of *Lightning Sharks*?"

Thelma nodded.

"The energy drinks?" Saman laughed. "Oh yeah, Thelma's addicted to them."

Thelma poked Saman, "You're one to talk. I haven't had any this whole trip."

"The first energy drink of all time," Bāne said, "The energy drink that led to all other energy drinks. Well, I invented them!" He leaned back and his tan, tattooed chest glistened in the sunlight.

Thelma's mouth fell open. "Really?"

Bāne nodded, "Yep, and as addictive as they may be,

Lightning Sharks are not good for you, but they're great for my bank account." He chuckled and stood, towering over them.

Thelma tried not to stare up his Hawaiian man-skirt.

"I need to say goodbye to the rest of my guests. Let's nap, then reconvene after sunset for dinner." Bāne left them sitting in the grass.

Thelma turned to Saman. "Have we lost our minds?"

Saman kissed her. "No. I feel saner than ever, and you've got to trust me and stop worrying about me."

Thelma blinked. "I... I wanted to make sure you were okay."

He took her hand. "I know, but you don't need to watch out for me like you're my secret service detail."

Her face flushed. That was how she acted. "You're right, I constantly worry about you. I can't help it."

"It isn't necessary, and it must also be stressful for you."

She nodded, "Okay, but don't you think Bāne's a little weird?" Thelma said. "And those girls he calls muses? It feels cultish."

Saman shrugged, "That's his lifestyle. Who are we to judge?"

Thelma frowned. "It's odd, and I'm surprised you want to stay. What did you see in the ceremony anyway?"

A wave of reflection passed over Saman. "I saw the universe and all my memories stuck inside a spider's web. My uncle was playing violin and my aunt was singing. When I concentrated on the music, the vibrations moved things through the web, to create space for the future. I saw you with your camera. The spider told me that I need to clear the pain from the past by living in an honest way, without any lies. That's why I wanted to tell you right away about the pain pills."

"That's very poetic and beautiful," Thelma said in a measured tone. "I'm glad you told me, and I'm happy Roberta is helping you, but we need to think this move through." She was happy to see him making progress, but the ceremony had delivered beyond her expectations, almost too far beyond them.

"Listen," Saman continued, "We'll rent out our house in Florida. I'm taking the hospital settlement, and with a salary and a free place to live, we'll pay off our mortgage. After this we can travel, open an art gallery, do whatever we want." He grinned, "We can even have a baby. I'm sorry for my reaction yesterday in the car; I knew I wasn't ready to be a parent, but I do want to create a family with you one day."

Thelma couldn't believe what she was hearing. "God, was that really yesterday?"

"Yep. Kind of mind blowing." He grinned.

"Are you sure you aren't still tripping?"

He laughed, "100% not tripping. Really."

"Thank you," she said.

"I mean every word."

Still in disbelief, but wanting to be convinced by her husband, she snuggled against Saman. *Maybe he's right,* she thought. *I need to trust him. If we stayed in Hawaii longer, I could also take that helicopter ride to see the volcano eruption and photograph the lava flow.* That idea excited her. Though Bāne's behavior was unsettling; there was something intimidating, almost inappropriate about him.

Saman stroked her hair like she was a child in his lap, "This will be the best thing that ever happened to us."

Thelma relaxed under his loving touch, "Okay babe, if this is what you want, we'll try it. I support you." As she said the words, an invisible tether, like a horse's lead, broke, and she let go.

19

I n her tidy examining room, Roberta, wearing khakis and a Hawaiian shirt under her white lab coat, patted Saman's knee. "Your bloodwork is great, and you started with the outpatient recovery group?"

"Yep, I really liked the people I met so far."

"Great. As you know, it's important for your recovery to stay connected and to connect with other people going through the same thing."

"For sure. I'm actually excited about therapy for once." Saman hopped off the doctor's examining table beaming, and shook Roberta's hand, "Thank you again."

"Just doing my job. You're the one doing the real work." Roberta turned to Thelma, "And your eye looks better, too. I'm glad you could see Dr. Khan."

Thelma nodded, "Yes, I'm so happy to be out of the eyepatch."

"I'm sure. Well, I'll catch you both around the house," Roberta said. "At least for another week, right?"

"Yep, and tomorrow we're going to the volcano park!" Thelma said.

"Oh, wonderful. You'll love it. It's my favorite place!"

"I want to visit the night observatory too sometime," Saman added. "Thanks again, so much for everything." He gave Roberta a big hug, causing the doctor to giggle.

They said their goodbyes and left the clinic. At Bāne's expense, they'd moved back into Roberta's cube house, while he got their new home ready. Bāne had also loaned them a pickup truck so they could return their rental Jeep.

Saman started the truck and leaned across the vehicle to kiss Thelma on the cheek.

"What was that for?"

"Because I love you." He squeezed her thigh. "Hey, let's stop by the beach on the way."

Thelma grinned, "Yes. I was going to suggest the same thing. We may as well enjoy ourselves before we start working."

"My thoughts exactly." Saman steered the pickup away from Hilo's town center and onto a tree-lined road, then curved to the east, gliding to the coast before pulling off to a roadside, rocky beach.

"I came here before," Saman said, as he parked the truck. "That day I brought you honey."

"It's beautiful."

Calmer today, the ocean lapped against the lava-rock-crusted shore. Overhead, without a cloud, the clear sky radiated a cool ultramarine blue. The same honey stand was off to the side, but now, two older Hawaiian women manned the shop, laughing and talking, sitting in front of the stall in folding beach chairs.

Saman turned to Thelma and touched her arm, "Stay here for a second." He jogged over to the honey stand. "Hi, ladies," he said.

"Hi. Would you like to sample some guava honey?" The

shorter of the two women gestured at the mason jars of golden liquid.

"I'll buy one." Saman passed her a fifty-dollar bill. Next to the honey on the counter was a basket of wrapped flower leis. He grinned and plucked a chain of dark pink flowers, "I'll take this too. Keep the change."

The woman raised her eyebrows. "Really?"

"Yep. I owe you. Have a great day."

Before they could respond, he waved goodbye and trotted back to Thelma with the jar of honey and the lei in hand, his jaunt so light and carefree that it bordered on skipping.

He handed his wife the honey and unwrapped the lei, then slipped the necklace of fragrant pink blossoms over her head.

"Oh, wow. This is beautiful," she beamed. "How sweet. No pun intended."

They both laughed.

"You're the sweetest," Saman said and hugged her tightly, "and the sacrifices you're making for us to stay, they mean everything to me. You mean everything to me."

"Oh my gosh, you are extra sweet today." Thelma hugged him back. "I'll always support and believe in you."

He cupped her face in his hand and kissed her on the lips. "I love you."

"I love you, too."

They released their embrace and strolled towards the sand.

"Hey, what are those guys doing?" Thelma asked, pointing to the ocean.

Saman followed her finger. The same men he had seen fishing were there again, in tank tops and baseball hats, with their small, white-sailed boat.

"Let's go see," said Saman. As they got closer, the two men turned around. Saman did not hesitate, he raised his hand high and waived, "Hello!"

This time, the men returned the greeting.

What are the chances? Saman wondered.

He reached the edge of the Pacific's endless blue horizon with Thelma. They found a deep tide pool, slipped off their flip-flops, and waded into the shimmering liquid. The beige sand felt like silk between his toes. He breathed in deeply and wrapped his arm around Thelma's waist, tethering her to him. They dropped into the warm waves, and held hands, letting the water wash over them, watching the men's little boats bounce on the azure sea.

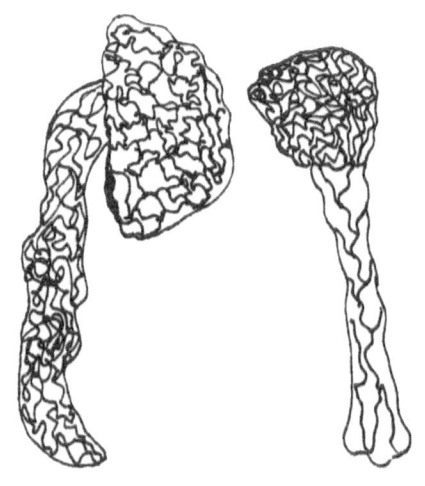

THE END

DEAR READERS

PLEASE REVIEW THIS BOOK

Thank you for reading! If you enjoyed this book, please leave a review on Amazon or Goodreads, or share this book on your social media and tag @CharlottDune.

Scan to leave a review on Amazon

Scan to leave a review on Goodreads.

Reviews help authors find new readers.

To read more from Charlotte Dune, subscribe to her newsletter here: http://charlottedune.com/contact/
or

Read and listen Charlotte Dune's Lagoon Podcast:

Charlotte Dune's Lagoon.
    https://charlottedune.substack.com/

ACKNOWLEDGMENTS

Thank you, Agah, for supporting me and taking care of my life while I went to Hawaii during the editing of this book. Mom, thank you for helping while I was away in Hawaii, and for being my early and observant reader. Thank you, Stephane, Gloria, Carlos, and Monica, for your impact on me. Thank you, Jeanine Elize and Louis Nathaniel, for bringing my characters to life visually and to Kyle, for helping me find an artist to further articulate my vision.

Thanks to my entire writers' support group, and especially to Lainey Cameron, for your help launching this book! Thanks, Heather Knorr for your help with the Spanish language and for your high attention to detail! What would I do without your eagle eyes?

Special thanks to Ann Kamoe, for all your help with corrections and suggestions for my Big Island wanderings, and to Tina Mahina, for your helpful ideas for my Hawaii trip.

Thank you, Ellen and David Kamoe also, for your enthusiasm about me going to Hawaii in the first place. You gave me permission to do something that I worried was too extravagant, and I love you both.

Special thanks also to Aya Kamanakai Iwasaki and to Porangui, for creating a retreat that allowed me to voyage to Hawaii while this novel was being edited. I never imagined I would actually go to Hawaii while I wrote this book, and I'm so grateful that I got the chance because of both of you.

Thank you for your inspiring spirits and the wonderful music, healing, and dance you create.

Thank you to all my readers and to friends who have supported me on this journey!

And a forever-thank-you to Neil Kamoe, who led my family to Hawaii in the first place. Your aloha is everlasting. You're always in our hearts.

ABOUT THE AUTHOR

Charlotte Dune is a romance, travel, and adventure writer based in South Florida. Her writing explores self-discovery, love, and exotic locations. She has a passion for travel, reading, nature, and expanding consciousness with entheogenic plants and compounds.

When not writing, you will find her by the pool with her partner, daughter, and their schnauzer, morkie, bearded-dragon lizard, and extra-large cat.

www.charlottedune.com

- facebook.com/CharlotteKDune
- twitter.com/charlotte_dune
- instagram.com/charlottedune
- amazon.com/author/charlottedune
- goodreads.com/charlottedune